The Devil Wears Timbs

A Novel by Tranay Adams

Email: trnayadams@gmail.com
Facebook: Tranay Adams
Cover design and layout by: Sunny Giovanni
Book interior design by: Sandy Barrett Sims
Edited by: Shawn Walker

Acknowledgements

Hey, you! Nah, not him, no not ol' girl either. You, the person that took a chance and purchased this book. Whatever the reason was for you picking it up at whatever book store or one-clicking it on Amazon.com. Thank You. You gave me a shot and that's all I've ever wanted. No handouts, just a shot. One measly shot. Good looking out, I appreciate it.

I'd like to give a shout out to The Jordan Downs Projects and The city of Watts in which the main characters in this book are from. Like my homeboy, Battle Rapper, Pro Aktive used to say 'On Young, Watts is like a whole 'notha state. Our walk, our talk, how niggaz move…we're different.'

Respect to my round Doe Boy, one of the realest breathing air. I love you my nigga, and I'm not 'bout to say No Homo. You know what it is with us.

Salutationz to Terry L. Wroten and No Brakes Publishing, I see you East Side, grinding and making them movez. We're from The Bottomz ain't no place else left to go but to The Top. I'll see you there, homie.

My hat's off to Author Godfather Wesley Hunter for offering me his wisdom and knowledge, respect, OG.

To my mother, Stella Ray aka My Old Lady aka the original Weezy F. Baby, I love you too death. You're the strongest person that I have ever known. You aren't a quitter and you didn't raise any either. I hope to make you proud of me one day. Wit yo nagging ass! Lol Love you, ma.

To my brother and my best friend, Tibbs, our bond is like no other. You always push me to go after whatever I desire. You always encourage me to do all of the thingz I wanted to do with my life. Let nothing or no one come between our union. We're all we got. I'd kill for you and I'd die for you. I Am My Brother's Keeper. This shit ain't just tatted on my arm.

To my Uncle Big Mac, I'll never forget the jewels you've laced me with whether it was on some street shit or manhood. Although, I was so young and innocent at the time you were giving me the game I still embodied it. You were right the life of a real nigga is a cold and lonely one.

My Big Cousin NeeCee aka Mamma Mia, I see you doing yo thang out here with them dinnerz. KANIGETAPLATE gone soar Loved One, you already gave it its wings. I can't wait to walk into Mamma's place or whatever you plan on calling your establishment.

If you're ever in the Los Angeles area hit my reli on her Facebook @Kanigetaplate. You won't be sorry, my peoplez getz down with the pots and pans.

Shouts out to the whole East Side, Low Bottomz, I grew up on the corner of Adams and Griffith, right across the street from ACE mini market, used to be Charlsey's mini mart (My Unc had that). Never forget my soil that's who I'm putting on for.

REST IN PEACE: Bryant Royal and Lymus 'Lil KB' White.

James Shelton Ray Grandfather, you're the only father I've known. Without you here this world don't mean shit to me. I see you when I'm done with my legacy, Love, Peace, and Respect.

Free Lil' Tip Toe. Richie Rich, Hold Yo Head, Flea! West Coast, Stand Da Fuck Up!!!

Dis My First Time Out The Gate, They Gotta Feel Me Or
They Gotta Kill Me!

THE DEVIL WEARS TIMBS

The greatest trick the Devil ever pulled was convincing the world he didn't exist.

Charles Baudelaire

Prologue

The night was as beautiful as it had ever been from the glow of the moon and the twinkling stars resembling crushed diamonds sprinkled throughout the black sky.

Raphael's was a very exquisite five star restaurant in West Hollywood off of the sunset strip. You couldn't get through the doors unless you were normally dressed and had made reservations months in advance. Its décor looked like it belonged inside of an 18th century castle with its white and gold fixtures. The painting on the ceiling was of Thor about to clash with the likes of Loki. The tables scattered throughout the establishment were covered with white cloths that were trimmed in gold with a gold candle holder sitting at the center of them. The windows were floor to ceiling and draped over them were gold curtains. A white marble dance floor was at the center of the room and a see-through glass bar sat off to the side.

The pianist's fingers moved like the waves of the ocean as he played the ebony and ivory keys of the grand piano serenading the scenery of the restaurant. Couples and lovers alike sat at their tables conversing or just gazing into one another's eyes. The waiters were busy throughout the establishment en route with entrées, filling champagne flutes, taking down orders, and pulling the corks out of wine bottles.

"You look nice tonight." Fear complimented his date from the other side of the table, taking a sip of wine.

He was a short dark skinned brother that rocked a close fade and a clean shaven face. Square diamond earrings hung from his earlobes and a Michael Kors watch adorned his wrist. He was wearing a gold Cashmere sweater and Versace loafers with Medusa heads on them.

"Thanks." Constance tried to conceal a smile. She was absolutely smitten by him.

Constance was a strikingly attractive woman with high cheekbones. She had hazel brown eyes and the sexiest pair of lips you'd ever seen on a woman. She wore her long thin, dreads pulled back into a tight bun. She was wearing a Badgley Mischka off the shoulder black form fitting dress, diamond earrings with a matching necklace, and a gold bracelet that looked like it belonged around Wonder Woman's wrist. The bracelet deserved to be in one of those glass display cases with an onyx plaque with some sort of inscription engraved on it inside of a museum of ancient artifacts. "I see a G got chu blushing over there." Fear flashed a sexy smile, showcasing all thirty two of his pearly whites.

"Whatever," she sucked her teeth, still unable to conceal her smile.

"Seriously, girl, you looking good enough to eat right now," he admitted. A nigga not used to seeing you like this. Normally, you're on that rah rah shit. Army fatigues and Timbs ready to bussa nigga head to the red gravy."

"I put the beast to bed for the night," she took a casual sip of wine.

"Talk that shit," he replied. "I tell you one thang, ma. The Constance with a purse and dress on is a lot hotta than the one with that banger in her hand."

"Is that right? Well, tell me which one you like best?"

"The one that's gon' have my back when we're in them streets," he answered. "There ain't no room for love in the life we live."

Hearing those words disheartened her, but she kept her game face on. She liked for him to believe that she was just as detached from her feelings as he was. But no matter how hard she tried, her true feeling always managed to break the surface.

"Live fast, die young." Constance uttered their mantra.

"That's right," Fear conceded.

2

"How are you lovely folks doin' tonight?" The waitress approached with a radiant smile, sticking a corkscrew into an expensive bottle of red wine. She was a redbone with a cute face and large bust.

"We're doing okay, how about chu—uh?" He looked closely at the nametag, trying to read her name.

"Brandi," she told him. "And I'm fine, thanks for asking."

Blip!

She clumsily pulled out the cork from the black bottle accidently spilling red wine on Fear's lap. He jumped up from his chair looking down at the stain on his Ferragamo slacks.

"Oh, my God, I'm terribly sorry," Brandi said, whipping out a cloth, "let me get that for you." She patted the wine from his crotch and slowly his dick print began to appear. Brandi gasped seeing his girth and length. "Damn, is that all you?" she questioned wide eyed.

Fear cracked a smile, peeling back his lips and boasting that million dollar kisser of his.

"Yeah, that's all me. But don't wake 'em up now, he might bite cha," he capped.

"I sure do hope so," she flirted, biting her bottom lip and eying him seductively.

Constance's face contracted with anger bunching the skin of her forehead and causing the skin around her nose to wrinkle. She was on fire and about ready to beat that bitch, Brandi, blind and bloody.

"Again, I'm sorry about that," Brandi apologized. "I'll get chu another bottle, on me."

"Don't worry about it, we're good," he waved her off. She was holding a bottle of Henschke Hill of Grace. That little black bottle was $500 dollars and he was sure that she wasn't clocking enough bank to foot the bill for it.

3

"Nah, we want another bottle," Constance insisted. "And this time can you send someone out that's not gonna spill the shit every goddamn where?"

"Relax," Fear gave her a look like *be easy.*

"I am relaxed," she gave Brandi the evil eye. The gaze coming from her was so intense you would have thought that Brandi was going to burst into flames at any given moment. "But she spilled the bottle of wine that you got for me on *my* birthday to go with *my* dinner. If that bottle's going to break her pocket, then oh well, maybe next time she won't be so clumsy, oh, daffy bitch." She kept those lethal eyes of hers on Brandi as she threw back the swallow of red wine in her glass.

Brandi stood there with one hand on her hip and the other gripping the bottle of wine. She was so heated that her face had turned a tinted rose red. She was wearing a scowl and a tight lip that she dared to spit venom out of like a poisonous snake. According to her watch, it was a quarter past her sticking her foot up Constance's ass.

"Oh, you still here?" Constance rolled her neck real ghetto like. "I guess you didn't hear me. Chop, chop!" She clapped her hands. "Hurry along now, servant, and fetch us another bottle of wine," she spoke as an 18th century king would to his royal subjects.

"Constance!" Fear said through gritted teeth, slamming his fist down on the table and rattling the dishes. The noise he made snatched the patrons' attention away from what they were doing. Seeing that all eyes were on him, he settled down.

She ignored his attempt to control her. The ladies held one another's gaze as Brandi talked shit under her breath before leaving to procure another bottle.

Fear leaned over the table locking eyes with Constance, "What the fuck is your problem embarrassing me in here? A nigga take you out somewhere nice and this is how you act?"

Tranay Adams

"Embarrass *you*?" She looked at him as if he had some nerve.

"Nigga, you the one over there flirting with this bitch," she began mocking him. *"Yeah, that's all me. Don't wake 'em up now, he might bite cha.* What the hell was that? Sex playing that skeeza in my face? You'za disrespectful ass nigga, *Alvin*," she called him by his government name. This was something she did whenever she was hot at him. "I gotta use the restroom," she shot to her feet, wiping her mouth with the napkin cloth and throwing it on the table. She rolled her eyes at Fear and headed to the ladies room.

Constance went into one of the available stalls. As she sat on the toilet to relieve her bladder, she gave herself a one on one.

I don't even know why you're tripping over some dick that doesn't even belong to you. Youz about a silly ass broad, Constance. You can't even be mad at Fear. He came at chu in a real way. He told you from the get go that y'all was just gon' be about getting this money and fucking from time to time. You acted like you could handle it, but chu can't. You fucked around and let that donkey dick nigga get chu open and you caught feelings behind him. What happened to you bitch? You used to be something beautiful. You used to get what chu wanted outta these niggaz and leave their asses stranded on the curb. Now look at chu, a love sick goddamn dog. Bend over so I can kick you in your ass!

After her pep talk, she concluded her bathroom routine and left. She journeyed down the hall feeling invigorated after taking the time to think things over. Rounding the corner, she saw something that made her step back and take a gander. Her eyebrows furrowed when she saw Brandi at their table. She sat the bottle on the table and jotted something down on her order pad. She tore the slip of paper from the notepad and handed it to Fear. After looking it over, he tucked it into his pocket.

5

Brandi walked away throwing that big old ass of hers from side to side with Fear watching every step of the way.

Constance leaned up against the wall in the hallway. She squeezed her eyes closed and sneered, balling her fists as tightly as she could. She fought back the anger and frustration coursing through her veins, tainting her blood. When she thought that rage had vanished, she opened her eyes and looked at her hands. Her palms were bruised red from her nails digging into them. Constance took a deep breath and turned out of the hall, heading back toward the table where Fear was seated.

For the remainder of the night, they talked and laughed forgetting about what happened earlier between she and Brandi, or so Fear thought. He called for the check, dropped two crisp big face hundred dollar bills for their meal and fifty for the tip.

He stood to his feet slipping on his black suede blazer. He extended his hand toward Constance, "Come on, ma."

"I gotta use the restroom before we leave."

"Again?"

"Yeah, I think it's the wine."

"Alright, I'll post up."

Constance picked up her clutch and rose from the table. When she noticed that Fear was no longer clocking her, she deceptively dipped off into the kitchen located nearby. She scanned the walls until she found where the timecards were. She quickly looked over them until she found Brandi's. *Bingo!* There it was. Brandi Gillard. She'd punched in at 2PM which meant she'd probably get off at ten o'clock that night. Constance stuck the timecard back into the space and returned to her table. Allowing Fear to lead her out of the restaurant, she locked eyes with Brandi who was placing entrées on another couple's table. The stare down was vicious and if looks could kill, both of them would have been laid the fuck out inside of that restaurant.

6

A few hours later, Fear was asleep on his stomach butt ass naked and calling hogs. Constance had put that pussy on him and now that ass was in a coma. Hearing him snore so loudly, she knew he wasn't waking up anytime soon which meant this was the perfect time to act. She mashed out the joint she'd fired up after sex and slid out of the bed, slipping her black thongs back on.

She moved toward the closet and pulled open the door. She didn't waste any time getting dressed and slipping on some Timberland boots. She tucked a pair of black leather gloves into the breast pocket of her red camouflage army jacket and stepped to Fear. She kissed him gently on the head and headed for the door, turning off the light as she disappeared through the doorway.

It was after eleven when Brandi came through the door of her house hanging up her purse and kicking off her flats. She pulled off her coat and threw it over the back of the couch. She picked up the remote control and turned on her 42" LG flat screen. She flicked through the channels until she found something that she wouldn't mind watching. Once she came across The Usual Suspects, she escalated the volume and tossed the remote control onto the coffee table. Brandi sang Drake's 'From Time' as she walked down the hall, unzipping the back of her skirt. She was about to walk into the bathroom when she noticed the window was cracked open at the end of the corridor. She frowned as she approached the window, closing it shut and then locking it. Thinking that she'd heard something, she froze where she was and her brow furrowed as she listened for it again.

"Humph." Brandi shrugged before entering the bathroom and flipping on the light switch. When the light didn't come on, she flipped it off and on rapidly. Nothing. Frustrated, she exhaled and stomped her foot. "Damn it. This light done blew out again? Shit!" she exasperated. This would have been the third time she'd changed the light bulb in the bathroom this week. She didn't know what the problem was, but she planned on calling an electrician to come out tomorrow since she didn't have to go to work the next day.

As soon as Brandi got the notion to turn around, something sharp jabbed her in the pupil. "Agh!" She held her eye as she staggered back into the hall and bumped into the wall. She opened her injured eye but couldn't see anything out of it, she had been blinded. Brandi touched her wounded eye and her trembling hand came away sticky with blood. Hearing a feral snarl, her head snapped up and she unleashed a scream so loud that her uvula shook at the back of her throat.

Chapter 1

"Sssssss, handle yo mothafucking business," Malvo hissed, looking at the top of Giselle's head as her juicy mouth slid up and down his short, fat dick. He swept the hair from out of her face and tucked it behind her ear. He slipped the same hand behind her neck and gripped it. "Look me in my eyes when you're sucking my dick," he ordered with authority, licking his chops and biting down on his bottom lip.

Giselle looked up at him with tears and eyeliner running down her face. Though Malvo wasn't that long, he had enough length to have her gagging. He scowled and his lips twisted. Veins formed in his neck and forehead. He could feel jizz rushing up his shaft and swelling up his dickhead. He slowly began to drive himself into her wet mouth. He couldn't wait to nut. Giselle's choking, accompanied by the sound of the saliva sloshing inside of her mouth, excited him. Malvo gripped the back of her neck tighter and sped up. The sensation of her mouth brought him to the tips of his toes.

"Old nasty ass bitch, you want a nigga to pop, don't chu?" Malvo asked exultantly, feeling his dick about to explode. "You want a brotha to bust all down yo mothafucking throat, huh? Fucking slut! Well, here it is." His thrust came faster, more aggressively and his face contorted into something monstrous. "Here it comes." Giselle pressed her hands against his pelvis to slow his stroke, but he smacked her hands down.

Gripping her head with both hands, he watched his dick jab in and out of her mouth. His eyes fluttered and rolled to their whites. Malvo hollered loud enough for the neighbors to hear him as he erupted and sent all of that creamy white baby batter down her esophagus. He thrust Giselle's mouth twice more, grinding into it before slowly pulling out his limp endowment. It was shiny and dripping with her saliva. The nut he had just bust brought a smile to his face and caused his body to shiver like he'd felt a cool breeze. Giselle wiped the jizz that dripped from the corner of her lips with the back of her hand, hurriedly. From the disgusted look on her face you would have thought that she'd tasted something putrid. She quickly rose to her feet and snatched a couple of napkins from off of the dresser. She was about to spit Malvo's jizz into the napkins until he spoke.

"Uh uh." Malvo shook his head from where he lay on the mattress clad in a doo-rag, a wife beater, and socks. He fired up a cigarette and blew out a cloud of smoke. "I wanna see you swallow that shit."

Still holding the napkins, Giselle got down on her knees before the mattress on the floor and Malvo sat up. "Ahh." she opened her mouth wide, so he could see the jizz cupped in her tongue. She swallowed it and a disgusted look crossed her face. She then used the napkins to wipe off her tongue and mouth.

"That's a good bitch." Malvo patted her head as if she were an obedient dog. He then looked around her bedroom for something to wipe himself off with. He scanned over the bedroom. There were small piles of dirty clothes scattered throughout the room and on the floor and overflowing out of the hamper. There was a nightstand sitting against the wall and one dresser which held a 20" square box television set. One of its dials was missing and it substituted a wire hanger as an antenna. It sometimes showed with a little static, but two whacks to the side of that old bastard would have its picture perfect.

Malvo snatched up a yellow flower dress from one of the heap of dirty laundry and cleaned off his shiny dick. Once he was done, he tossed the stained flower dress aside.

"You got that for me?" Giselle asked impatiently as she twiddled her fingers.

For a time Malvo didn't say a thing, he just sat there smoking his cigarette and observing her. She sat with her ass on the soles of her feet in anticipation for that packet of salvation he could only give her. Looking upon Giselle, he couldn't help to feel like he was the master of a Golden Retriever.

He remembered a time when Giselle was one of the baddest bitches to have ever worn a pair of pumps. She had tits you could press up against glass, and an ass you could sit a 40 ounce bottle of liquor on. Her face was one to marvel and her body made a brother want to sing a Keith Sweat ballad. Back in the day, Giselle Gabriella Jackson was stamped a certified dime. Malvo had always lusted after her. He'd spent most of middle school and all of high school chasing her, but she didn't have any holler for him. She was cup caking with this square cat by the name of Bootsy, and she wasn't giving any other brother the time of day.

Malvo was relentless in his pursuing of Giselle. He wouldn't stop until she belonged to him. Although, he couldn't have her, he'd abide his time so that he could in the future. Miraculously, his time came when Bootsy was murdered in cold blood late one night on his way home from work. His death had brought about Giselle's vulnerability and yearning for companionship. She knew him from back in the day, so there wasn't a problem for them to become reacquainted. He showed up at her front door one night with a packet of something special to relieve her pain and a stiff one for her to slob on. It took some convincing, but eventually she relinquished her power to his advances. It wasn't like she could help it. She was weak, distraught and in turmoil. She was ready to try just about anything to ease her grieving. So, when he offered her equanimity in a small packet labeled 'Kryptonite' she renounced her better judgment.

"I don't know, Malvo. I don't want to get strung out." *Giselle said one night while sitting on the living room sofa,*

staring at the packet of Kryptonite in her palm. The lights were dim and Marvin Gaye's 'Just to Keep You Satisfied' serenaded them.

"You won't get strung out, baby," Malvo lied in his sexiest voice, combing his fingers through her hair as he gently caressed her thigh. His breath was warm against her earlobe and the slight brush of his lips caused her pussy to tingle. "I won't let that happen, I'ma take good care of you. You're my lady now." He placed tender kisses up her neck. "You want to feel better, don't you?" she nodded as she wiped the tear that trickled from her eye with a curled finger. "Well, this will make things all better. It'll whisk you away from all of the ills and heartache of this world to a euphoria all of your own."

Thinking of how much her heart ached at that precise moment, Giselle wanted to visit this place that he spoke of. If it was really that enchanted, then once she got there she knew that she'd never want to leave.

"Okay. Alright." Giselle nodded her head rapidly.

"You sure?" Malvo asked between putting hickies on her neck and pulling one of her breasts free from her blouse.

"Yes, I'm sure," she rasped, feeling the warmth of his wet tongue as it lapped and sucked on her areola. He brought his head back up. Their tongues did a dance and then their mouths massaged each other.

Malvo plucked the packet from Giselle's palm and prepared a shot of dope. After tightening his belt around her arm, he smacked her forearm until a vein appeared, then picked up the syringe. Bringing the syringe toward the vein, he looked up into her eyes and cracked a grin, giving him the appearance of a snickering rodent that had just cleverly snatched a pebble of cheese from a mouse trap. He kissed her lips one last time before administering the shot. Once he was done, he released the belt from Giselle's arm and capped the *syringe, sitting it on the table. He watched as she was granted entrance to the euphoria he'd spoke of.*

"Ummm," she moaned and licked her lips. Her eyes fluttered as she groped her breasts. Her reaction to the dope was kindred to that of an orgasm. Malvo rubbed her thigh, allowing his hand to travel near the warmth of her treasure.

"That shit feel good to you, baby?" he asked in that sexy voice of his.

"Ye...yes...baby," she uttered, experiencing the ecstasy that the drug brought.

"Well, get ready, baby, 'cause I'm about to make you feel great," he swore, whipping his Glock from his waistline and laying it down on the coffee table. He got down on his knees and pulled her to the edge of the sofa. He slipped her panties off and tossed them aside. He then rested her legs on his shoulders. Malvo and Giselle's pussy were face to face like two fighters at a weigh in. He French kissed that pussy and sucked on that fat clit of hers, sensually. Giselle squirmed under him, moaning and groaning in delight. I got this mothafucka now, he thought.

From that day forth, Malvo had been in there like swimwear. He'd ridden Giselle from the sexy young stallion she was then to the walking cadaver she was now. He knew she wasn't what she once was, but she had a shot of head and a snatch that was a blessing from God. On top of that, her apartment doubled as his stash spot. He kept his work hidden there while he crashed at his crib out in Westwood. Giselle knew exactly where it was but she'd never touch it because he kept her high. Not to mention, if she dared to fuck with his product, he'd hack off the very hand that she'd stolen with.

"Yeah, baby, hand me my jeans over there." Malvo pointed toward the nightstand that his jeans were sprawled across. Giselle threw the jeans to him and he fished inside of the pockets until he found what he was looking for, a packet of that infamous Kryptonite heroin. She scrambled over to the dresser and pulled open the drawer. She grabbed all of the utensils she needed for her fix. She snatched the packet from Malvo's palm and got down to business. He slipped back into his clothes. After putting on his sneakers and sweatshirt, he watched as the heroin took Giselle from the misery of this world and into the bliss of the next. A slight smirk formed on his lips. He knew that as long as he had good dope, she would be his just as long as he wanted her.

*****

Eureka was lying on the filthy, raggedy tan sofa. One leg was stretched across the cushions while the other dangled off of it. One hand was gripping the back of the sofa while the other held the remote control as she flipped through the channels of the old square box television set.

Eureka was a mahogany brown skinned chick with sleepy eyes that made her appear high 24/7. She had a head full of dark curls and a cute baby face. She was only nineteen, but carried herself with the aura of a woman twice her age. She had a pinch of tits and wide hips that protruded to thick juicy thighs.

Eureka was the prize of The Jordan Downs projects. All of the niggaz from around the way yearned for her, trying to get a sample of her young goodies. She was looked upon as a trophy being that no one from the courts could say they'd had their way with her. Eureka had dudes coming out of the pocket and rolling out the red carpet for her. She would pretend like she was giving a dude some play long enough to get what she wanted out of them. And then, within the time span it took to snap your fingers—she was gone.

Eureka's head shot up from the sofa when she saw a figure walk by through the openings of the blinds. She waited to see if the image would cross the next window, but when it didn't she had a feeling who it was and what they'd come to do. She unchained and unlocked the door, then snatched it

14

open. She came face to face with the resident manager, Mr. Rifkins. He was a short, portly man with arms too little for his body. To most, he looked like a dwarf but in actuality he just wasn't very tall. Eureka looked from him to the sheet of paper he'd taped to her front door. She disconcertedly snatched the paper down, fearing what it was but already knowing at the same time. She'd been through this several times before, but that didn't stop her stomach from doing summersaults. She'd never get used to it no matter how many times it happened. That would be like waking up every morning knowing that you were going to get shot. It could happen a hundred times but you'd never grow accustomed to it.

Eureka glanced at the sheet of paper. She didn't have to bother with reading it all because she knew its contents by heart. It was an Eviction Notice. All occupants of the unit had three days to pay or leave the premises. *Fuck*, she thought to herself. She already knew what had happened. It was the familiar struggle of her mother having used the rent money to purchase drugs once again. "Old Giselle's back at it again, huh?" Mr. Rifkins lifted his trucker cap from off of his head and scratched his balding scalp.

He knew Eureka and her fifteen year old brother's situation all too well. When their father, Bootsy, had been murdered three years prior, their mother became a heroin addict. This left her in charge of the household. She took on the brunt of the responsibility doing the best she could with what she had and sometimes pulling off the impossible. Mr. Rifkins had no idea how she was going to pull off this miracle. He sympathized with her, though. He really did. He tried to pick up the slack whenever she couldn't by pitching in the couple of dollars that they'd needed to make rent or inviting them over to he and his wife's apartment for dinner. He wished that there was something that he could do, but this time his hands were tied.

"Yeah, Mr. Rifkins, I don't know what I'm going to do with her." Eureka blew hard and shook her head as she clutched the paper, tightly. She shifted the weight of her body to the other leg and tapped her foot, heatedly. She was so angry with her mother she could smack a spark out of her.

"Alright, well, I'll keep you all in my prayers."

"Yeah, send them prayers up, 'cause we sho' nuff need 'em."

"Alright, now."

"You have a good one, Mr. Rifkins." She waved him off as he headed across the courtyard to his apartment. The portly man threw up a hand and went on about his business.

Eureka slammed the door shut so hard that it rattled the portrait of her family hanging on the wall causing it to fall. Upon impact, it cracked into a spider's web. Almost like an omen, signifying that her family, too, had been broken. She headed down the hallway seething with hot tears cascading down her face. She punched her mother's bedroom door in passing and then disappeared inside of the bathroom, slamming that door shut as well.

Eureka stared at her reflection through the dirt smudged medicine cabinet mirror. A roach hurried across the mirror, but she didn't pay it any mind. She stared into her worrisome eyes and watched the tears escape down her cheeks. Slowly, her face transformed into something ugly as she sobbed. Feeling as though she'd become too loud, Eureka cupped her hands over her mouth to muffle her cries. Her head slightly bobbed the harder she wailed. But then something came over her and suddenly she stopped. The look in her eyes was as if she'd seen something behind her. She gripped the sides of the porcelain sink and peered into her reflection, looking at herself like she didn't know who she was. She wiped her wet face with the inside of her shirt.

"Look at chu, bitch, in here bawling like a goddamn baby?" Eureka shook her head, shamefully. "What would daddy think if he saw you right now? Pull yourself together, ma," she coached herself. "You're a gladiator and this crazy world is your arena."

Eureka took deep breaths, inhaling then exhaling repeatedly to calm her jittery nerves. She turned on the faucet, cupped her hands under the running water, and splashed her face twice. It seemed to have helped cool the heat scorching beneath the surface of her flushed skin. *Get it together,* she thought. Wiping both hands down her face, she sloshed the dripping wetness away. Feeling invigorated, she stepped out of the bathroom, but froze in her tracks when she saw Malvo sitting on the sofa, reading over the wrinkled Eviction Notice.

Malvo's eyes shifted up when he heard the squeak of her sneakers against the worn flat carpeted floor. He cracked a devilish grin and sat the paper down on the coffee table. "I see we have ourselves a situation," he mentioned casually.

"That's none of your fucking business and I'd like you to stay outta my family's personal affairs." Eureka snatched the source of her looming headache off of table, folded it up and tucked it into her back pocket.

"I can make all of this go away if you do a little something for me," Malvo eyed her seductively.

"I already told you, I don't get down like that," Eureka said with an attitude, folding her arms across her chest.

Malvo had cracked for the pussy on several occasions and each time she had turned him down. He had offered her everything from money to expensive jewelry in exchange for a taste of her sweet nectar, but she wouldn't take the bait. He figured a poor little ghetto girl would easily drop to her knees for the material things he dangled before her, but he had her pegged wrong. Eureka wasn't some hood rat that got gassed whenever a couple of dollars was waved in her face. A man was gonna have to come with far more than that if he wanted the keys to her mansion.

The Devil Wears Timbs

"Now, you see there? Your mind's in the gutter and all I'm trying do is put chu onto making some paper, so you can keep a roof over y'all heads."

"I'll put it to you like this, homeboy," Eureka began. "If it has anything to do with me sucking and fucking for it, then I'm not even tryna hear that noise. Like I said before, *this* pussy and *this* mouth are not for sell, capeesh?"

"It's not even that kind of party, sweetheart," Malvo took a drag from the cigarette, "All I need for you to do is take a lil' trip out of town for me."

Eureka extended a hand, gesturing toward his smokes. He gave her one of the cigarettes and took the liberty of lighting it for her. He then tossed the lighter on the table and lay back on the sofa, continuing with his spiel. She contemplatively smoked the square while halfway listening to Malvo's proposal. "You make this run out of town for me and I'll drop fifteen grand in your lap."

Hearing fifteen thousand dollars made her perk up. He had her undivided attention now.

"Fifteen racks, huh?" Eureka said ardently, scratching her chin with the hand she held the cigarette in. The mention of all those dead white men had her captivated. But she needed to know the specifics before she agreed to make the run. "I take it I'm transporting dope," she made her assumption. Malvo smiled as he blew smoke ringlets into the air. His devious smirk confirmed it, she'd guessed right. "Okay, what I need to know is how much dope I'm moving?"

"Ten kilos."

Eureka was in her thoughts as she paced the living room floor, taking casual pulls from the square. *He wants me to move ten keys of blow for fifteen stacks. That ain't jack shit compared to the risk that I'm taking. If I get caught up, I'm looking at a football number. If I do this, it's gotta be worth my while. We're gonna need food, clothes, a car, and beds for me and Ant. Shit, with enough dough I could move us up outta*

18

The Bricks and send mommy to a decent rehabilitation center.
Fuck that, this nigga gone have to break a bitch off more than
fifteen grand if he wants me to bust this move.

Suddenly, Eureka stopped pacing the floor and turned around to Malvo. "You want me to run ten kilos out of town?" she asked rhetorically. "Alright, cool. I can do that, but you're gonna have to come up off of a little more than fifteen racks."

Malvo blew smoke out of the side of his mouth as he mashed his cigarette out in the ashtray. He repositioned himself on the sofa and steepled his hands together. "Give me a number," he locked eyes with her.

"Forty," she matched his intensity.

"Forty?" He shot to his feet and shooed at the air as if to say, *Get the fuck out of here.* "That sounds preposterous. Come again."

"Nah, Big boy, there ain't no come again," Eureka said seriously. "If you want me to make this trip, I need forty, or you can find yourself another mule."

Malvo massaged his goatee as he weighed his options. He had a couple of degenerates that he was sure he could get to make the trip, but they may not be able to slip past the authorities. He felt comfortable with Eureka because she was a female. It was a known fact that women were less likely to get stopped by the police than men were. He decided to chalk up the extra twenty-five grand as the cost of doing business. It was in his best interest to let her make the run, so he'd get a return on his investment. He stood to make a couple hundred thousand, so forty grand wasn't going to hurt his pockets.

"Okay, lil' momma, I'ma give you a play. I just gotta run and pick up this Grey Hound bus ticket. Come tomorrow morning, I'ma strap you up and ship you out."

"Alright, but I'ma need a hundred and thirty dollars to cover my rent today," she held her hand out, wiggling her fingers in anticipation.

Malvo shook his head at Eureka's take charge attitude. He was able to respect that about her. He peeled off a few bills and placed them in her hand. She counted them and ensured that they weren't counterfeit. Seeing that the money was all there, she slipped it into her bra. *Problem solved,* she thought.

Tranay Adams

Chapter 2

The entry bell chimed as soon as Anton crossed the threshold of Reggie's Liquor & Junior Market on 104th and Central Avenue. He was on his way down the candy aisle whistling Dixie when he felt someone watching him. He looked over his shoulder and grimaced at the store clerk who was mopping the floor and watching him like a hawk in the sky would his prey. Anton stopped in his tracks and swiftly turned around.

"Damn, Bull, what are you mad dogging me for?" Anton asked as if he really didn't know why.

"I know that was your lil' ass that clipped me for that case of booze last week," Bull said with a twisted face. He was a dark skinned, husky cat with nappy cornrows and a face full of acne. He rocked a smock over a white T-shirt and a pair of New Balance sneakers. "You try lifting something outta this bitch again and I'ma break yo ass off something real proper like, ya hear?"

"Whatever." Anton waved him off and went about his business, "Ain't nobody gotta steal nothing outta here. I got money," he capped.

Anton's stomach's grumbling sounded like the angry roars of a thunderstorm. He hadn't eaten since earlier that morning. That egg sandwich had come and gone. Hell, he had shitted that out hours ago, so he was back on E.

Anton knew that he didn't have any business going to the Reggie's that day. He was as hot as coal there. The only reason he hadn't hit up any other store in the area was because the owners had threatened to shoot him on sight if he stepped into their establishment again. Anton figured he'd be better off taking his chances at Reggie's. He reasoned that the most Bull would do was beat his ass and he could handle that. An ass whipping was a lot better than a chest full of lead. He had

22

stolen everything that Reggie's had in stock at one time or another. If he wasn't stealing something to eat, then he was shoplifting something to sell so that he could eat.

Anton eyes swept up and down the racks of candy. He looked up and saw Bull watching him through the slight opening in the aisle. He sighed and shook his head. He didn't know how he was going to pull this heist off under his watchful eye. Just then, the clouds parted and the sun shined on his ass. A customer came through the door and shared a few words with Bull, thwarting his attention away from him. Anton didn't waste any time grabbing as much junk food as he could, stuffing it into his pockets. He was so hungry that he ripped open a pack of Twinkies and crammed them both inside of his mouth. His jaws worked overtime as he made a beeline toward the exit. He had almost made it through the door when a strong hand suddenly yanked him backwards.

"Fuck you going?" Bull asked, grabbing Anton by the back of his shirt and shaking him violently. His teeth were clenched so tightly that you could see the skeletal bone structure in his jaws. "What did I tell you, Sticky Fingers? Didn't I tell you not to come in here stealing shit?" he admonished.

"What chu talking about, man. I don't have nothing," Anton tried to break free. But the cream residue from the Twinkies around his mouth was a dead giveaway of his deceit. Bull had hemmed him up so far off of the floor that the tips of his sneakers barely touched the surface. Bull was a much stronger man, easily outweighing him by a hundred pounds.

"Say, man, I'm outta here." The irritated customer abandoned his items at the counter and headed out of the door. Bull didn't acknowledge the angry patron. Anton was his sole focus.

Holding Anton around the collar of his now stretched out shirt; he went about the task of running through his pockets. "You ain't got nothing, huh? Fuck is this?" He yanked out candy bar after candy bar, letting them fall at their feet. His pockets looked like bunny ears after Bull was finished empting them, turning them inside out.

"Youz about a thieving ass lil' nigga." Bull shoved him, but Anton rebounded and cracked him in the mouth with a sharp bow. Bull stumbled backwards and fell against the potato chip rack, falling to the floor along with it.

"Bitch ass nigga!" Anton spat heatedly with both of his fist clenched. Though he was a little nigga he was about a million miles down the road from 'Bitchville'. You could give him directions and he still wouldn't know how to get there. "There ain't no pussy here, homie. These are balls," he grabbed the bulge in his jeans.

Bull lay on his back on the floor grimacing and groaning. He slowly stood to his feet, wiping his bloody lip with the back of his hand.

"That's yo ass, boy!" his forehead creased and fire danced in his eyes. He was hotter than a pistol with five murders on it. His hands balled into fists and he charged Anton like he was a matador.

****

Fear took the occasional toke from his cigarette as he studied the photograph of the cat he was supposed to kill. He wondered what his life had been like before he took to the streets. Just because he was slinging crack didn't mean he was born in the ghetto. He could have been raised in the suburbs and came from a good family, like himself.

See, Fear was brought up in a Christian faith based, two parent home as an only child. He was an academic genius and lived a square life. It wasn't until the summers spent in the Eastside of Los Angeles that he was able to live outside of the rigid lines drawn by his strict folks that he developed a taste for excitement. His cousins Wakeem and Malik stayed in a

24

section of the trenches nicknamed, The Low Bottoms. It was there that he became educated in The School of Hard Knocks. Fear got an up close and personal look at all of the things he'd read about in a CA$H novel or had seen in movies like Boyz n the Hood and Menace II Society. Mesmerized, he rebelled against his parents wanting him to finish his education and succumbed to the allure of the streets. Needless to say his parents weren't happy about it so they kicked him out of the house.

With no place left to go, he took it back to the Eastside to hustle with his cousins. They soared to predominance in the crack game, but took a few loses. Wakeem and Malik caught life sentences. With them out of the picture, Fear was left to maintain the rise of their empire. Although, Fear was sitting on the throne, he wasn't *that nigga* yet. He knew that he was going to have to make some power moves if he wanted to be Top Dawg. He was seeing a lot of money but knew that he'd see lots more if he got rid of the opposition. Without remorse and with extreme prejudice, he had his competitors whacked but left the smaller operations alone. However, he did give them an option *either buy their drugs from him or die.* Outnumbered and outgunned, the smaller operations didn't have a choice but to bow down to an entity greater than them.

Fear experienced an influx of wealth and notoriety. He was deemed a street king and niggaz gave him a wide berth. Mothafuckaz came to realize two things. They either paid homage or got a dome full of hollow-points. His reign was a long and prosperous one. He ruled his hood with an ironclad fist. But as the saying goes, "All good things must come to an end."

Detective Broli approached Fear with a file loaded with enough evidence to bury him and his organization if he didn't give up his plug. Fear, being the standup nigga that he was, told Broli to suck his dick when Broli decided to move forward with the dismantling of his empire.

25

But he thought better of the situation and offered him an alternative. One million dollars, every penny he had to his name in exchange for his freedom. Once Broli got the money, he did exactly like he told Fear he was going to do. He set him free and burned the evidence he had on him. Knocked right back down the totem pole, he was forced to start over from scratch. His days of trapping were left behind for new trades. Now, he made his grips as a stickup kid and contract killer. He made far less, but it garnered him a decent living.

Fear mashed out his cigarette in the ashtray and removed his sleek, black .32 from the console. He chambered a round into the head of the pistol and screwed a silencer onto its barrel. He hopped out of the '76 Buick Regal and hustled across the street to handle his business.

*****

Wop! Wop! Wop!

A three punch combination rocked Anton and dropped him on his ass. Bull stepped back with his left foot forward and fists up ready for the third round.

"Uh huh, you gon' learn today. I'ma beat the brakes off dat ass." Bull swore, dancing around like a skilled boxer.

Anton touched his lip and his fingers came away bloody. Seeing the blood seemed to incite the fighter inside of him, he growled as he came up from the floor, tackling Bull and lifting him up off of his feet. He slammed his elbow into Anton's back until he released him. He then grabbed him by the shoulders and kneed him in the gut, knocking the wind out of him. Anton dropped down landing on one knee bracing himself with the steady of his palm against the floor, wearing a mask of hurt. Bull kicked him in the temple and his head pounced off of the freezer door. He hit the floor on the side of his face, teetering between consciousness and unconsciousness.

"Pussy," Bull hocked up phlegm. He slightly tilted his head back as he was about to spit on him when he was caught off guard.

Whack!

Splinters flew everywhere as the handle of the mop was swung against the back of Bull's skull. He stumbled forward and crashed to the linoleum. He turned over from where he lay looking through a haze of pain at his assailant. He saw three blurred images before him. When the images united and his vision cleared he saw Eureka holding a broken mop handle. Luckily for Anton, she had to get a money order for the rent, otherwise, she wouldn't have been able to intervene and that would have been his ass.

"Don't you ever put your hands on my brother, bitch!" Eureka stared Bull down and tightened her grip. She widened her stance, ready to crack that ass again. "Are you alright, Ant?" she asked without taking her eyes off of him.

"Yeah, I'm okay, sis." He slowly stood, rubbing his head.

"You gon'—" Bull wobbled to his feet, holding his busted dome. His head was aching and he was blinded by pain. "You gon' get it now, bitch. You done fucked up." He grabbed a hold of the counter to balance himself. He struggled to stand, his legs felt like cooked noodles underneath him.

"I hear you talking, but step this way and I'ma take ya funky ass head off of ya shoulders." Eureka swore, praying that Bull would try to call her bluff so she could send his head out into orbit.

"Oh, I got something for you, stay ya monkey ass right there." Bull reached behind the counter holding his head and his gaze on Eureka. When he came back up he was clutching a pretty ass silver .357 Magnum revolver. Seeing the pistol made Anton tense up, but she held fast to her gangster.

"Oh, you wanna pull a strap, ol' punk ass nigga?" Eureka said. "Well, blast then. Let me see some of that G shit you claim you 'bout."

"You gon' respect my gangsta." Bull cocked the hammer back as his finger settled against the trigger. Eureka lifted the broken mop handle and was about to launch it in his direction when Fear stepped between her and the barrel of the pistol.

"Whoa! Whoa!" Fear said, holding up both hands. "What's the problem here?"

"This doesn't concern you, so breeze." Bull nodded his head toward the exit.

"Or the coroners will be zippering up three bodies instead of two."

"Slow ya roll, bruh. I'm not tryna see nobody murdered or nobody going to prison," Fear claimed. "Now I'm sure all of this can be resolved. What exactly happened here?"

"You wanna know what happened, Mr. Good Samaritan?" Bull asked but didn't wait for him to answer. "That lil' pipsqueak there has been robbing me blind for the past month and I'm sick of it. He tried to pull that shit today and I caught 'em red handed. After I gave 'em what he was due, that hood rat behind you cracked me upside the head with that fucking mop handle." He took his hand from his head and saw that it was masked with blood.

"Lil' man, is this true?" Fear asked.

"I was hungry." Anton shrugged like it wasn't a big deal. "A nigga gotta do what he gotta do to eat, feel me?"

Fear nodded his understanding. He then turned to Bull and pulled a healthy knot from his pocket. He licked his thumb, counted off ten bills and dropped them on the counter.

"Check it, family. I want you to take them there marbles and put it toward getting that head of yours patched up, okay?" Bull looked at the thousand dollars Fear had dropped on the counter and then back to him. He thought on it.

He could get that gash in his head stitched up at County General for free and pocket that money. Bull hesitantly lowered his pistol and snatched the money off of the counter. He still wanted to give Eureka and her thieving brother the business, but money talked and bullshit walked—at least for now it would.

"Okay," Bull agreed.

"Lil' man," Fear addressed Anton.

"What's cracking?" He threw his head back, still mean mugging Bull.

"Grab yourself some groceries," Fear generously offered.

"Man, I'm broke as a joke," he patted his empty pockets.

"Don't worry about that, family. I got chu faded."

"Why are you doing this?" Eureka asked once her brother had left to retrieve the items.

"I'ma sinner, lil' momma, hopefully this good deed will reserve me a place in heaven," Fear responded.

"What're you looking at?" She caught Bull shooting daggers at her.

"Whatever I damn well please," Bull retorted. He then yelled to the back of the store. "Lil' nigga, hurry up so y'all can raise the fuck up outta my store," he pulled a rag from his back pocket and patted the gash on the back of his head.

Anton returned and begrudgingly placed all of the items on the counter.

Bull glared down at him as he rung up the items, "That's forty-seven dollars and twelve cents, ya thieving lil' fucka."

"Nigga, suck my dick." Anton threw up the middle finger.

"Chill, Ant," Eureka told her little brother. She looked to Bull, laying a few dollars on the counter. "I need a hundred and thirty dollar money order, too."

29

Fear gave Bull a new big face hundred dollar bill. Bull slid Eureka her money order and handed Fear his change. Fear turned his hand palm up and smacked the loose bills and coins into it, closing it up.

"That's you, family," he told him.

"Thanks," Anton said.

"You're welcome," Fear gave him dap.

"Could I have your name and number, please?" she asked.

Lines formed on Fear's forehead and he threw his head back slightly, "Why? What's up?"

"I just wanted to get your info, so I can pay you back," she told him.

"You good, it's on me."

"Uh uh." Eureka shook her head. "We don't accept charity, so if you'd please shoot me that info."

"No charity. I respect that," Fear nodded. He borrowed an ink pen from Bull and jotted his name and number down on the back of the receipt. He passed it to Eureka and she looked it over before sticking it in her pocket.

"Thanks. And I'm going to pay you back," she said, shaking Fear's hand.

"I know you will. What are your names?" he asked.

"I'm Eureka and that's my little brother, Anton," she answered.

"Alright, Eureka, y'all take it easy."

"Thanks again," Eureka and Anton made their way toward the exit.

Bull groaned as he touched the rag to the back of his head. He looked to the blood on the rag and it made him angrier. "Lil' half pint mothafucka done busted my shit open," he said to no one in particular. He then looked up at them, mad dogging them as they were leaving.

Tranay Adams

"You better grow eyes in the back of your head, Leprechaun," Bull hollered at Anton. "'Cause this shit here is far from over."

"You better know it, homeboy," he shot back. "It's on sight, that's on mommas."

Eureka threw her arm over his shoulders and ushered him out of the door.

"You're something else you know that?" Bull addressed Fear. "What is your reason for looking out for them street rats?"

"There's more evil than good in this world. I'm just tryna restore the balance." Fear looked up at the variety of liquor on the shelf behind Bull, narrowing his eyes, "Let me get a fifth of Hennessy, a box of Magnums and a pack of Newport shorts."

Bull sat all of the items on the counter except the cigarettes. He reached above his head to take the pack down. When he brought the pack down, his eyes bulged and his mouth dropped open seeing death stare him in the eyes.

Choot!

The low whisper of the silencer hushed the bullet that entered Bull's mouth and exited out the back of his neck. He fell up against the shelves causing a chaotic crashing sound of breaking bottles dropping to the floor as he slid down in a slouched position. He sat slumped staring off to the side into the dark gaze of The Grim Reaper. Fear stepped around the counter and deposited two into his chest. He relieved him of the money he'd given him earlier and the freezer bags full of white crack he knew he kept stashed beneath the floor board. Once he cleared Bull's trap, he grabbed the video surveillance tape and made a beeline for the exit.

The Devil Wears Timbs

Chapter 3

Eureka opened up the freezer and grabbed a tray of ice. She dumped the ice into a freezer zip-loc bag. She then handed it to Anton who was sitting in the chair licking his busted lip.

"What's this for?" He looked at the cold compress.

"Hold it to that knot on the side of your head."

"I'm straight, I don't need that."

"Take the bag, tough guy," Eureka insisted.

"Nah, I'm good, sis."

"Anton," she shot him a look that he read, *You better take this shit.*

He sighed and reluctantly snatched it from her. He held it to his head and touched his lip, checking to see if it was still bleeding.

"You alright?"

"Yeah, I'm good. Ah," he hollered after she punched him in the chest. "Fuck was that for?" He rubbed his sore chest.

"For having your black behind out there stealing," she told him. "If I hear about chu being out there again with the five finger discount, I'ma break the same hand that you used to shoplift. You hear?"

"I was hungry. I had to do what I had to do to eat."

"You could've come to me. I had a couple of dollars for you to get something to eat with."

"I'm almost a grown man. I'm not gonna depend on my sister to feed me. I'ma go and get it like my Daddy taught me."

Eureka smirked and ruffled his hair, "Don't rush to grow up, baby brother. Stay a kid as long as you can. You have only but so many years to be a child but all of your life to be an adult."

"It's too late for all of that, sis. The Bricks turn lil' boys into men."

Eureka thought on it for a second. What he had said was so true to life that she didn't have a witty remark to come back with. All she could do was nod her head in understanding.

Eureka busied herself putting up the groceries. Once she was done, she sat a chair before Anton and straddled it backwards.

"Guess what?" She beamed brightly.

"What's up?"

"I got the rent money," she held the money order up before his eyes.

Anton snatched the money order from Eureka's pinched fingers and looked it over. He then gave it back to her asking, "How did you come up with the loot?"

"I made a deal with Malvo."

"Sis, I know you ain't give that fat bastard no…"

She threw up a hand, cutting Anton short.

"The day you see Eureka Jackson selling ass is the day you're going to see Jesus walking through that door," she nodded to the front door.

"Then what's the deal?"

"She gotta run ten kilos of heroin outta town to Oakland for him." Giselle interjected from the doorway, taking tokes from a square. Her hair was pulled back in a ponytail, showcasing her makeup free face. Hard living and hard drugs had made a thirty-three year old woman look like she was fifty-five.

"You're running Dog Food for Malvo?" Anton looked to Eureka with raised eyebrows. "And, mommy, you're letting her?"

"What chu mean *is she letting me?*" she asked. "I'm nineteen years old."

"Sis, if you get popped with that much weight, its curtains." Anton stressed the seriousness of what she'd planned to do as if she didn't already know. "That'll be it for you and them crackas will make sure you never see the streets again."

"You think I don't know that, Ant?" Eureka unstraddled her chair. "I don't wanna do this, but we need the money," she reasoned.

"You don't have to move Malvo's dope. We can make ends meet ourselves. I can go to work mowing lawns with Victor and his father, and you can see what's up with your old job at Mickey D's or you could go back to working for Spoons."

Eureka looked down, exhaled and shook her head. She looked back up at Anton and said, "Baby boy, Spoons is not letting me sling for him no more. His ugly ass baby momma got jelly and had him cut me loose. He claimed he let me go 'cause he didn't have enough to pay me and his other workers, but I know what bullshit smells like. Ol' girl always had an attitude and something slick to say about me. I know it was her that fucked up my check."

"You should have whipped that ass," Anton told her.

"What? You ain't know?" She outstretched both of her fists. They were riddled with teeth marks and fresh scabs.

"Okay, what about Mickey D's? That nigga, Gill, loves your dirty drawers. I know he'll let chu get your gig back. You were only suspended 'cause you were late a couple of times, right?"

"I got fired."

"But you said…"

"I lied to you, Ant," she interrupted. "They fired my ass for stealing outta the cash register. They could have had The Ones lock me up, but Gill convinced 'em to let me walk."

"Damn, sis, I don't know," he said, not wanting her to make the run.

35

"I know, I know. It's risky, but Daddy got my back."

"You really think Pop is up there looking out for us?"

"How do you explain us making it through these past three years?"

"True. I guess there's no way that I can talk you outta making this run." He looked into her eyes, hoping she would say there was something he could do to persuade her.

"No," she shook her head. "I do what I do for this family, for all of us."

"Alright then, when are you supposed to leave?"

"Tomorrow morning."

"A'ight," Anton walked into the living room and plopped down on the couch. He picked up the remote control and flipped through the channels, looking for something to watch.

"Come here, baby girl," Giselle motioned her over.

"What?" Eureka stepped forth.

She hugged her daughter, taking her off guard. She then kissed her on the cheek.

"What was that for?" The line in her forehead deepened.

"Stepping up to the plate. I know you're putting your neck out on the line for our family, and I appreciate it. Thank you."

"You wanna thank me, Ma?" she asked. Giselle nodded *yes*. "Then get clean and start being a mother to your son. That's one thing that I can't do."

"I will, baby. I will."

Eureka left the kitchen and headed into her bedroom.

******

Eureka walked inside of the bathroom and closed the door shut behind her. She twisted the dials and a spray of hot water erupted from the showerhead. Steam impregnated the bathroom and fogged up the medicine cabinet's mirror. She kicked off her Timberland boots, pulled off her tank top and peeled off her tie dyed jeans. She drew the shower curtain back and stepped into the tub. Once she'd gotten good and wet, she picked up a bar of cheap soap and began lathering up. Her mind drifted to Giselle.

She hadn't been much of a mother to her and Anton since their father was murdered. Ever since his passing, Eureka had been taking care of them. She felt like she was more like his mother than his big sister. And truthfully, she was. Giselle was too busy getting off on Johns to support her habit to be any kind of mother to either of them. So, it was up to her to make sure they kept a roof over their heads and something hot to eat. It for damn sure wasn't easy, but she took the bull by its horns. While most teenagers in her position would have buckled under such pressure she took the responsibilities on without complaint.

Eureka turned off the water and stepped out of the tub. Once she had dried off she hung the towel up on the towel holder. She slipped on her panties and rubbed a clear circle into the mirror, so she could see her reflection.

A smirk formed on her lips as she stood in the mirror rubbing her upper body with baby lotion. Her small hands traveled over her shoulders and arms. Eureka loved her body. But as beautiful as it was it had its flaws. She turned to her side, rubbing down her arms as she studied the hideous scars on her back. She frowned seeing the keloid welts overlapping one another, traveling from her shoulders down to the lower half of her back. Running her hands over the welts, she felt like a blind woman reading brail.

Eureka thought back to the day she'd gotten the keloid welts.

Anton had stolen this local drug czar's Yukon truck by the name of Kilo. He took the truck to the chop shop and walked away a few hundred dollars richer. He would have gotten away with it if it wasn't for his stunting through the

37

hood in it earlier that day. Some of everybody had seen Anton in the truck clowning, so when Kilo offered five stacks for his whereabouts niggaz started pointing fingers.

A day later, Eureka came home from her gig at McDonald's and found Anton being pistol whipped by Kilo. She pulled the razor blades from her mouth that she always carried around in case someone tried her on her way to and from work. She tore into Kilo like a feral alley cat, slicing up his face and making it resemble a game of Tick Tack Toe. Kilo left that day in an ambulance with his shit leaking. Two weeks later, Eureka was knocked out cold on her walk home from work. When she woke up she was hanging from a meat-hook in the freezer of an old meat market. There to greet her was Kilo with a leather whip.

Kilo whipped her for five days and five nights. When he got tired of whipping her, he'd piss on her, spit on her, douse her with bleach, and mashed blunts out on her. Left for dead in the meat market's freezer, Eureka wrestled her wrists from the bondage of the rope. Half naked with a raw bloody back, she ran all of the way home. When she was admitted into the hospital, the police came asking questions but her lips were sealed. She stayed true to the code of silence that she was taught growing up in the hood.

A week later, Eureka was released from the hospital. She was lying on her stomach in bed watching TV when she heard a knock at the door. When she opened the door, there wasn't anyone there. Only a purple Crown Royal bag sat at her feet. She scooped up the bag and carried it into her bedroom. She sat on the bed and pulled the bag open. She dipped her hand inside and pulled out a gold Cuban link chain attached to an icy 7" capital K. The link and the K were speckled with blood and tiny pieces of brain.

Later that night in the courtyard, niggaz were drinking, smoking, and discussing street politics. Eureka was just about to close her window when she heard one of them mention Kilo.

"Y'all didn't hear about what happened to that nigga, Kilo?" one young man asked.

"Nah, what happened?" A second young man inquired.

"Nigga, they found that nigga slumped in his car with four in his knot."

"Damn, somebody did my nigga filthy." A third man declared.

"On Young."

Eureka wasn't sure who had gave Kilo the business, but she knew for a fact that it was in her honor. Getting Kilo's blood stained chain delivered to her doorstep was proof of that. Eureka had a few people in mind being that a lot of folks in The Bricks had love for her, especially the OGs from around the way. At first she wasn't sure who it was that had flat lined Kilo, but something told her that it was Anton who had put in that work. When she asked him, he swore up and down that he didn't have anything to do with it and chalked it up to bad karma. She didn't press him any further. She just thanked him and kissed him on the forehead.

Eureka slipped on a wife beater, basketball shorts and tied a doo-rag around her head. After cracking open the blinds to allow the dim illumination of the street lights to shine inside of the bedroom, she hopped into the sofa bed they shared.

On Eureka's side of the bedroom were posters of AV, Ty Dolla $ign, Nipsey Hussle, August Alsina and Trey Songz. On Anton's side of the bedroom were posters of Meagan Good, Lauren London, Tika Sumpter and Regina Hall. There was one dresser with five drawers they shared. Two of the drawers were missing their fronts, making the clothing in them visible. On top of the dresser was a 32" flat-screen Eureka had gotten from her days of hustling for Spoons. The walls inside of the bedroom were once white but had turned beige over the years from sweating during the sweltering summers. A 20" osculating fan stood in the corner. Its face was missing and its blades were caked with dust. An old black stereo missing some of its dials and buttons sat on the floor below the window. The Jackson kids didn't have much, but they cherished what little that they did have.

Eureka tossed and turned in bed trying to find a comfortable position to go to sleep in. Giving up, she turned on her back and clasped her hands behind her head. Suddenly, the door opened and Anton walked inside. He sat on the end of the sofa bed and kicked off his sneakers. He pulled his shirt over his head and stripped down to his boxers. He then lay back in bed and threw the sheets over his person.

"Sis?"

"Watts up?"

"Nothing, I thought that you were probably asleep."

"Nah, I can't sleep for shit."

"Me either."

There was a hush between them as they both had become tangled in their thoughts. Anton spoke up, breaking the air of silence in the room.

"You ever miss, Daddy?" he asked.

"Every second of every day, and every minute of every hour."

"Me too."

"Man, if Daddy was alive we wouldn't have to worry about shit," Eureka assured. "He always made it happen. Even after he fell off, he was still out there pounding the pavement making ends meet."

Bootsy was a bus driver at MTA until he got fired for a fight with a disgruntled passenger. When he lost his job he hit rock bottom. He was forced to take his family from a four bedroom, two bathroom house in the suburb of Calabasas to a two bedroom one bathroom in the Jordan Downs projects. Bootsy went from making $72,000 dollars a year to $20,000 dollars a year busting his hump at a warehouse gig. He made shit pay, but he was able to get by with his hustling a little weed on the side.

Although, The Jacksons were forced to down grade significantly, Bootsy still kept smiles on their faces. Bootsy was the pillar and foundation of his family. Even when the chips were down, he seemed to always manage to come through for them. Bootsy was a miracle worker. He made sure his family had all of what they needed and sometimes even the extras. They may have not possessed all of the luxuries that they had before, but they had the most important thing in the world and that was each other.

"Real life."

"Don't worry about it though, 'cause I'ma fill Daddy's shoes." Eureka assured her sibling. "I got us."

"Nah," Anton sat up in bed, looking at Eureka. "We got us. You think I'ma just be sitting on my ass while you're tryna make it happen? Daddy would turn over in his grave. He taught me better than that."

Eureka sat up in bed, locking eyes with her brother. She extended her hand and said, "A and E, we all we got," she said on her Nino Brown shit.

They gave each other a complex handshake.

"Now, let's get some sleep. I gotta get up early in the AM," they both turned over in bed and snuggled under the covers.

Eureka had just closed her eyes when her nose wrinkled. "What the hell is that foul smell?"

He laughed and giggled, "My bad, sis."

"Ah, nah, lil' homie, you've gotta catch my fade." Eureka clobbered Anton with her pillow. He grabbed his and clobbered her back. They jumped to their feet in the bed and went swing for swing, in a no holds barred pillow fight.

They spent the remainder of the night laughing and playing around until The Sandman appeared and swept them away.

Tranay Adams

Chapter 4
The Next Day

Malvo was leaned over in a chair inside of The Jackson's kitchen. He rifled through a Macy's shopping bag where he had ten blocks of heroin hidden underneath beach towels. One by one, his hands came from out of the bag holding blocks of heroin wrapped in tinfoil and beige tape. He stacked the blocks neatly on the table on top of one another. He picked up his smoldering cigarette from out of the ashtray and took a quick pull. He then reached into another Macy's shopping bag and pulled out a hefty bubble coat, baggy blue jeans, and an L.A. fitted cap. Malvo was grateful that it was the month of October because the weather was cooler, making the warm clothing justifiable. And Eureka would need hefty apparel to hide the dope he was going to strap her down with.

He blew out a roar of smoke and glanced at his titanium Rolex watch, wondering what was holding Eureka up.

"Lil' momma, what's taking you so long in there?" Malvo called out to her. "Come on and let's get this shit done. I got things I gotta do."

A moment later, she emerged through the doorway clad in her bra and panties. She was uncomfortable being partially naked in front of him and watching him molest her with his eyes made her skin crawl. She was becoming vexed at his ogling of her.

Goddamn, girl, your moms ain't got shit on you. Lil' sexy, young bitch. I bet that pussy tight as a choke-hold.

A fiendish smirk appeared upon Malvo's face as he imagined himself putting the dick to her. He felt his fuck muscle shift in his jeans becoming semi erect. He wanted a shot at that warm wetness between her legs, but it was business before pleasure with him. Sitting up, he blew out a cloud of smoke and mashed his cigarette out in the glass ashtray.

"Come here." He motioned Eureka over with a wave of his meaty hand. "As long as you took, you're gone mess around and miss the bus." Malvo spread her arms and legs apart. He hurriedly went about the task of duct taping the kilos to her body. He'd gotten nine of them packed on her when he realized that he didn't have any more visible spaces left. He immediately jerked her panties down around her ankles.

"What the *fuck?*" Eureka pushed him away, knocking him on his ass as she pulled her panties up. "Negro, what the hell you think you about to do?" She frowned, preparing for a fight if he took it there.

Malvo raised his hands in the air as he stood up, "Relax, lil' momma, I just need to stash this other joint." He licked and sucked two of his fingers, lubricating them with his saliva.

"You thinking about jamming that brick into my insides? Uh uh," Eureka shook her head *no*. He had her fucked up. "That ain't gone happen, captain."

"Come on now, my people are expecting ten joints," he reminded her.

"Well, they're only gon' be getting nine this trip." She spat with sass, hands on her hips and neck rolling like a chicken head.

Malvo took a deep breath and brought his hands down his face. He was so hot that you could fry an egg on his forehead. He wanted to put hands on Eureka, but he didn't want to rock the boat. He needed her for this trip. He had a lot riding on it. Malvo knew that he'd fair better keeping a cool and calm head so he suppressed his anger and took a different approach.

"Look, lil' momma," he began. "Business has been good between me and these folks. And I'm not tryna do nothing to fuck it up, ya feel me?"

"I can respect that, but ain't nothing being stuffed between my cunt muscles," she stated earnestly, standing her ground.

"Man, fuck that!" Malvo went to pull Eureka's panties back down and she smacked him across his face. The assault came so abruptly and so hard that it left her hand stinging and caught him by surprise. A small red hand impression was left on his right cheek.

"Youz about a hardheaded bitch, you know that? Now, I told you that I wasn't letting you stuff that heroin into my pussy. If you don't like how this train is moving, then maybe you should get off at the next stop," she said with a hard-face, watching the fire dance in his eyes and his nostrils flare. Malvo's face twitched with anger.

They stared each other down like a couple of old western gunfighters. The silence was broken when they heard her mother's voice.

"Reka, is everything okay in there?" Giselle called out from the living room where she and Anton were sitting on the couch watching television.

"Yeah, ma, everything is fine," she answered, keeping her eyes on him.

"Are y'all almost done?"

"Uh huh," she replied, still watching him. "So, what's up? Are we going through with this or what?"

"Yeah, we're still going through with it," he looked upon her with derision.

"Okay then, let's finish this up," she said.

Malvo snatched the Glock from his waistline. He grabbed Eureka by the neck and forced her up against the wall, pressing it into her eye. He burrowed into her eyes as his finger settle on the trigger. The two of them were out of sight just enough for Giselle and Anton not to see them.

"The next time you put your hands on me, I'm gonna put a bullet through your eye, ya hear me?" he asked behind a scowling face, clenching his teeth.

That didn't unnerve Eureka. Growing up in the projects, she'd seen worse and had even worse happen to her.

"You keep your dick tuggers to yourself and you won't have to worry about me putting my hands on you." She tightened her jaws. She knew that Malvo wouldn't hesitate to make good on his threat, but she'd let her nuts hang anyway. She was a straight up G behind hers and would die for her respect. "Now, let's wrap this shit up. I gotta bus to catch."

Malvo held Eureka's gaze a few seconds more before shoving his piece back into his waistline. He then grabbed the roll of duct tape from off the table and motioned for her to turn around. Forcing a space on her where he could strap the last kilo, he rolled out a length of duct tape and pulled it apart with his teeth. He held the kilo against the tight but exposed flesh and taped it down.

Once Eureka had gotten dressed, he made her model for him. His arms were folded across his chest as he tilted his head from left to right looking at her from different angles. He narrowed his eyes trying to see if there was something that was off about her appearance. He thought that she seemed normal enough, but he needed to make sure so he called Giselle and Anton into the kitchen.

"Y'all take a look at lil' momma and tell me what y'all think," he asked of them. "Do you notice anything off about her?"

Giselle was clueless as to what she was looking for, but she examined her, nonetheless.

"She looks just like one of those manly looking dyke bitches." Giselle scratched and peeled open the scabs that trailed the course of her arm. "Besides that, I don't notice nothing outta place."

"I'm not worried about her looking like no butch. As long as she can weasel her way around them cops at the Greyhound station, I could care less what she's perceived as." Malvo took a sip from his glass of Hennessy. "What chu think, lil' nigga?" He looked to Anton who eye fucked him and headed out of the kitchen. "You eyeball me like that again and I'ma snatch them bitches outta ya head, ya hear?" he threatened.

"You touch me or my brother and me and you are gonna have a situation," Eureka warned.

"Whatever," Malvo said, not trying to get into it with her again. "Do you think you can make it past them boys and get on that bus?"

Eureka nodded and said, "Yeah, I can do it."

"Alright then," Malvo said to no one in particular. He threw back the last swallow of Hennessy left in the glass and grabbed his leather jacket from off the back of the chair. "Come on, girl, we've gotta bus to catch."

He held a hand to Eureka's back as they headed out of the kitchen.

They'd almost crossed the threshold when Giselle called him back.

"What chu want? I'm on a tight schedule now." He glanced at his watch.

"Ain't chu gon' throw me a lil' something to hold me over 'til you get back?" She scratched her neck. His brows furrowed as he shook his head, looking down on her resembling a dog with fleas. Malvo reached inside of his leather jacket, pulled out two packets and threw them at her feet. He watched Giselle scramble to the floor for them before she ran off into her bedroom, slamming the door shut behind her.

"Let's get outta here." Malvo led her through the living room.

"Hold on." Anton hopped off of the sofa and embraced Eureka lovingly. "I love you, sis."

"I love you too, baby boy."

Breaking their embrace, they gave one another a complex handshake that they ended by snapping their fingers.

"Good luck."

"Thanks."

Malvo clapped his hands and said, "Alright now, come on, come on." He ushered Eureka through the front door.

She rode in silence in his '94 Chevy Caprice classic, staring out of the window.

Dear God, please let me make this drop without a hitch, as you know, me and baby bro have been through a lot these past few years. Times were harder than Chinese Arithmetic and sometimes I thought that we weren't gonna make it, but we prevailed. I ask that you watch my back on this mission. I know that what I'm about to do is wrong, but like Grandma Betsy used to say, don't ask for permission ask for forgiveness. Amen, Eureka thought. She then crossed her heart in the sign of the crucifix.

Malvo listened to Curtis Mayfield's *Pusher Man* and smoked a cigarette as he drove through the Los Angeles streets. Occasionally, he'd glance over at Eureka. He could tell from her reflection in the window that she was worried, and she had every right to be. If she was busted, the only way she'd be getting out of prison was inside of a body bag. The weight of the world was on her shoulders and the only way it would be lifted is when she'd reached her destination and unloaded the drop.

"You nervous?" He turned down the stereo, looking between the road ahead and Eureka. She looked to him, exhaled, and nodded slightly, *yes.* "Don't worry about it. When you get there you waltz right into the place like your shit don't stink. Like you're Queen mothafucking Elizabeth and the rest of them mothafuckaz are your royal subjects," she nodded, but it didn't lessen her concern. "And if all else fails, here's a lil' something, something to take the edge off." He plucked a neatly rolled joint from his breast pocket and passed it to Eureka. He watched as she examined the joint and sniffed it. She looked to Malvo and he smiled and winked at her. She stuck the joint between her full lips and punched in the cigarette lighter. "Whoa, you're not finna get fucked up now. If you go strolling your lil' ass into that station high outta your mind, The Boys are sure to stop you once they get a whiff."

"Right." Eureka took the joint from her lips and stashed it inside of her coat.

"This cat you're supposed to connect with down in Oakland is called Stretch," he informed her. "This nigga got east Oakland on smash. He's a low-key millionaire and shit. Anyway, you're to call him up once you make it to the motel. That reminds me. Here." He pulled a burnout flip cell phone from his jacket's pocket and passed it to Eureka. "There's only two numbers in there. That's mine and Stretch's. You'll place two calls to me. One to let me know that you made it and one to let me know that the drop was made, you got it?"

"Yeah, I got it." Eureka nodded her understanding.

"Now, Stretch may or may not bring this broad named Fat Fat with him," Malvo said. "Sometimes he brings her along to test the dope to make sure it's potent. But for the most part, you shouldn't have anything to worry about. I've known this dude for a minute now and he's always done square business."

"Is there anything else that I should know?"

"Yeah." Malvo scowled as he placed his Glock on his lap. Eureka looked it, then back up into his eyes, unfazed. "If you don't return with every dollar of my money accounted for, I'm going to execute your mother and your brother, one by one. I don't wanna hear any stories about you getting jacked, extorted by crooked cops or none of that shit. If you can't come back with my trap, then you may as well stay where you are and make the funeral arrangements from there."

"Are you threatening me?"

"Yes, I am," he admitted, tucking his Glock inside of his leather jacket.

"Hopefully, I won't have to make good on it."

He cranked the stereo back up.

Eureka sat in silence the rest of the ride to the station, staring at a mangled picture of her, Anton, Giselle and Bootsy that she always carried. Her life seemed so surreal back then. Everything was picture perfect. She had the ideal family. The one you sat around on the couch and watched on television. People around the neighborhood thought of The Jacksons as the ghetto version of The Huxtables.

"We're here." Malvo killed the engine and hopped out of the car. Eureka stashed the picture of her family inside of her coat's pocket and stepped out. She made her way to the rear of the car and found him removing items from the trunk. Inside, there was a suitcase and a duffle bag of clothes too big for her to fit. It didn't matter, though. Seeing how she wasn't going to be wearing them anyway. She was to use the duffle bag and the suitcase to transport the money back. The clothes were inside to throw off anybody looking to stick their nose in her business.

Malvo peeled off a couple of Dead Presidents from his sizable bankroll, passing her three one hundred dollar bills.

"That's a lil' something for ya pockets while you're out there," Malvo told her. "Don't ever go anywhere without no paper on you." His eyes shifted up from hers and spotted a quartet of sheriffs standing beside the entrance. "Looks like you've got the welcoming committee awaiting your arrival." He nodded in the direction of the sheriffs. When Eureka glanced over her shoulder and saw the cops she swallowed hard. "Aye." He snapped his fingers and brought her attention back around to him. "Remember to hit up Stretch as soon as you get to the motel. Once that exchange is made, you hit me on the jack, alright?"

"I got this," she faked confidence.

"Alright then, that's what I'm talking about," Malvo smiled and held out his fist. "Show me some love."

Eureka allowed his fist to linger in the air for a moment before giving him dap. Malvo playfully punched her in the shoulder and then watched as she made a beeline for the Greyhound station's entrance. At her rear, she heard a car door slam shut and its engine start. She then felt the wind as the car blew passed her. She didn't even have to look over her shoulder. She knew it was him who'd sped out of the parking lot. He was putting as much distance between himself and The Greyhound station as possible. He didn't want to be caught anywhere near the shit storm if Eureka was busted. She couldn't blame him though because if it were her, she'd be getting the fuck out of dodge, too.

Eureka's feet seemed to grow heavier and heavier with each step she took toward the station's entrance. She'd gotten about ten feet away from the doorway when time seemed to slow down to a snail's pace. Her footfalls sounded like those of a giant each time her Timberland's touched the surface.

She noticed the sheriffs were having a conversation amongst themselves as she approached. One of the sheriffs, a tall white stud with a bushy dirty blonde mustache, casted his baby blues in Eureka's direction. The sheriff narrowed his eyes and peered closely. There was something about her that intrigued him. He didn't want to believe that he'd seen what he'd saw, but his instincts told him otherwise. He wanted to go after her, but he needed to be sure his eyes weren't deceiving him. He had to be a hundred percent sure before he made his move. Eureka was scared shitless. She felt the sweat trickle down the back of her neck and the palms of her hands growing damp. Her heart rate was jacked, and each of its beats felt like a .44 Magnum revolver being fired internally. But all of those emotions were playing on the inside. On the outside, she held a game face. She grinned and nodded to the sheriff as she crossed his path, but he kept a suspecting eye and a tight lip.

Once she crossed the threshold into the station, she thought she was in the home stretch. A smile stretched across her face and she felt a sense of accomplishment, and just that fast her world went spiraling out of control and crashing.

"Hey, you!" the bushy mustache sheriff called after her.

"Fuck me!" she cursed. "I knew it, I fucking knew it."

"Stop, goddamn it!"

Eureka felt the sheriff coming up behind her and she put a little pep into her step. She gripped the duffle bag and the suitcase tightly and sped walked.

"Shit!" Eureka spat, seeing the reflection of the sheriff on the waxed floor as he hurriedly bopped up behind her. She knew that it was all over then. She was just about to drop her bags and breakout into a full sprint when a strong hand grasped her shoulder, jerking her around.

"You think you're pretty fucking slick, don't cha?" The sheriff said, wearing a devilish grin knowing that he'd foiled a wicked plot.

"What?" she faked ignorance. She looked over her shoulder and saw the rest of the sheriffs approaching. She panicked on the inside but kept her game face, still.

"I could smell it on you the moment you crossed my path," the sheriff told her.

So, this is how it's gonna end for a bitch? Nabbed before I even step foot on Oakland soil? she thought.

Woof! Woof! Woof!

Eureka's head snapped to the left and saw the rest of the sheriffs approaching with German Shepherd police dogs on leashes. The dogs barked and snapped at her viciously. She reasoned that they could smell the heroin on her even though Malvo took the liberty to mask its odor.

The Devil Wears Timbs

She could hear her conscience screaming at her, *what the fuck are you waiting for, bitch? Get the fuck from out of there! Run! Run! Goddamn it, run!* She wanted to take off but her legs wouldn't cooperate with her for some reason, so she decided to stand there and take her medicine. "Excuse me, but I don't know what you're talking about."

"You don't know what I'm talking about, huh?" The sheriff looked at her like *'You know exactly what I'm talking about'*. "Well, what's this?" he drew her bubble coat open and felt like the biggest Jack Ass on the planet. What he believed was a chrome pistol was actually the silver flip cell phone that Malvo had given her clipped to her belt.

"Uhhhh, uh…" The sheriff was speechless as he scratched his temple.

"Since when it is a crime to have a cell phone?" she asked.

One of the other sheriffs stepped forth and said, "We're sorry about that, Miss. You're free to go."

"Apology accepted." Eureka looked upon the sheriff that had stopped her like the dumb ass that he'd proven to be before going on about her business. She could hear the other sheriffs chastising him as she walked away.

"Robinson, you dick," one of the sheriffs said. "I really thought you had something there."

Eureka ducked off inside of the Women's restroom and locked the door behind her. She carried her bags to the stall at the far end of the restroom. Stepping inside, she locked the door behind her and sat on the commode. She fished around inside the pocket of her coat until she produced the joint Malvo had given her. With a trembling hand, she placed the joint between her lips. She then patted herself down for a lighter. Her hand brushed across a lump inside the pocket of her jeans. She reached inside and pulled out a book of matches. She struck a match across the black strip at the back of the match book and it came away pregnant with a flame.

54

Eureka wasted about four matches before she was able to successfully light the joint. Her hand had been quivering so badly that it shook off the flame of the match. Eureka sucked on the end of the joint until she felt herself mellow out. Once she became accustomed to her indulgence, she lay back on the commode. Her eyes had slowly begun to close when she heard a rattling at the door that shot her eyes open. She quickly sat up from where she was perched, looking around as if she didn't know where she was.

"It's occupied."

The door rattled again from knocking.

"Someone's in here," she grew agitated.

The door rattle some more.

"I said, *fuck off*!"

The knocking ceased and Eureka went back to lounging and partaking in the joint. She smoked a little less than half of it before mashing it out against the wall inside of the stall and sticking it inside of her bubble coat. She then snatched up her bags and left the restroom. She was now on her way to East Oakland, California with calmer nerves.

Chapter 5

The sun's rays felt like the dull tips of one hundred needles pelting against a sleeping Eureka's eyelids. She stirred awake. First, wiping the scum from out of her eyes and then sitting up. She yawned and smacked her lips coming from out of her slumber. Stretching her arms, she heard her bones readjusting and her back cracking into place. Eureka looked ahead just in time to see the sign *Welcome to Oakland'*. About a half an hour later, the bus pulled into the Greyhound station. She gathered her bags and hustled off of the bus. The first thing she did was call Malvo to let him know that she'd made it to The Bay. The line rang twice before he answered. "Speak on it," he came on the line.

"I made it," she replied.

He disconnected the call.

"Mothafucka," she said of his rudeness, flipping the cell phone closed and clipping it to her belt.

She looked up and narrowed her eyes as she was blinded by the sapphire in the sky. Eureka held a hand over her brows and took in the scope of her surroundings. People were procuring the awaiting taxis and going off to their destinations. Eureka spotted one last taxi. She'd started for it when a man in a business suit, toting a briefcase and a newspaper hurried over and hopped into the backseat. Behind the window glass of the backseat, the man looked in her direction wearing a guilty expression. He knew he was dead ass wrong, but fuck it he had places to go and people to see. Eureka's brows furrowed and her mouth twisted, she was hot. She went to give the man a piece of her mind. When old dude saw her heading in his direction he unfolded his newspaper and buried his nose into it. She had almost reached the curb when the taxi drove out of the parking lot.

"Bitch ass nigga, you knew that was my ride." Eureka hollered at the back window of the taxi where the man looked out smiling and licking his tongue out at her. Eureka held up the middle finger at the man until the taxi merged into the city's traffic. She looked over her shoulder and saw a pair of sheriffs at the rear of their cruiser holding cups of coffee. Their eyes were on her the entire time the fiasco unfolded.

Oh shit, she mouthed with bulging eyes.

The presence of the law caused her stomach to twist into knots. She'd forgotten all about the ten kilos of heroin strapped to her body. Eureka picked up her bags and went on about her business. She'd taken about two steps when she heard a voice at her rear.

"Baby girl, you need a ride?"

Eureka turned around to find a sixtyish fair skinned man wearing a jovial expression. A toothpick was at the corner of his mouth and his body was leaning to the right resting all of its weight on a redwood cane. He was sporting a fedora, a dingy Mickey Mouse T-shirt under a vest and worn penny loafers.

"I might," Eureka said with attitude. The old head standing before her didn't look like any taxi driver she'd ever seen. He looked more like one of those old niggaz who took time up in front of the liquor store drinking cheap liquor out of brown paper bags and shooting the breeze.

"Where to?"

"A motel, some place real affordable," she said.

"I know just the place, come on." He waved her on and limped toward his vehicle. He took five steps before he looked over his shoulder and saw that she wasn't following him. "Well, do you want a ride or what?"

Eureka folded her arms across her chest and shifted her weight to her right foot, looking at the old head sideways.

"Are you really a taxi driver?"

"Yeah."

"Then where's your car?" she asked suspiciously. Eureka wasn't anybody's fool. For all she knew this cat was some old pervert looking to abduct her and keep her locked away in his basement to perform all kinds of wicked sex acts on her. The next thing she knew she'd be in the thick of human trafficking, being purchased as a sex slave.

"Oh, it's right there." He pointed to a money green '87 Buick Regal.

Her brow furrowed and she shot the old head a disbelieving look.

"That's your taxi?"

"Yep," the old head said, as he removed his fedora and patted the beaded sweat from his forehead with a handkerchief. "Kenny G's Car Services. I'm just getting it off the ground, but we'll be up and running like a well-oiled machine in no time. Just gimmie about two or three mo' years, I'll have a fleet of exotic cars and more than enough able bodies to drive 'em. You just watch and see what I tell ya."

He seemed like he was legit, but Eureka still wasn't too sure about him. That story he'd given her could have just been game. Whether the old head was laying down G or speaking from the heart, she had to salute him because he sounded sincere. Nonetheless, Eureka's main concern was getting out of the sun and washing the day's stench off of her. She planned on grabbing a motel room, taking a hot shower, and calling up the cat she was supposed to pawn the heroin off on. She wanted to get the business out of the way as soon as possible, so she could catch the next Greyhound back home. Throwing caution to the wind, Eureka took a deep breath, exhaled, and decided to take a chance.

"Alright, come on," she said.

Kenny G smiled and exposed the gold crowns on his front teeth. He dropped her bags into the trunk of his car and held the door open for her. Once she was inside, he slammed the door shut and hustled over to the driver side. He fired up the old Regal and rolled out of the parking lot.

Eureka looked around the interior of the Buick Regal. He was stitched into the back of the seats' headrests. A small chandelier hung from the ceiling and the floor was covered by mink carpet. A pair of furry dice hung from the rearview mirror along with a solid gold crucifix. In the dashboard there were pictures of a young Kenny G suited and booted, flashing money and surrounded by beautiful women. The rest of the pictures were of who Eureka assumed were Kenny G's children and grandchildren. The décor of the car and the pictures confirmed it for her. He was an ex-pimp.

"So, what brings you to The Bay?" He gnawed on the toothpick and stole a peek at Eureka through the rearview mirror.

"Business."

"Business?" he grinned. "What kinda business do you have? You don't look a day over fourteen."

"I'm nineteen, thank you," she shot. "And my business is all my own, I suggest you find you some to tend to."

"You've got some mouth on you to be but so big."

"It's not about the size of the dog in the fight, it's about the size of the fight in the dog."

Kenny G chuckled and said, "You know what, baby girl, I like you. You remind me of my granddaughter."

"That's what's up," she said. "You mind if I smoke in here?"

"Long as you let me get a toke or two."

Eureka nodded and stuck the other half of the joint between her lips. She cupped her hand around her mouth as she brought the burning match stick to the end of the joint. The end of the joint glowed ember and she took a few puffs, fanning out the match. She then passed the joint up front to him and sat back in the seat.

"Y'all gotta CVS or a Rite Aid out here?"

"Sure do."

"Stop there first. I need to pick up a few things."

"You got it."

Kenny G made a left at the next light en route to Rite Aid.

*****

Kenny G posted up beside his Buick eating a bag of Planter's Cashews and watching Eureka. She was down on her knees, covering her mouth with his handkerchief he'd given her and spraying a cap-gun black. She sprayed the cap-gun once, shook up the can, and began adding the second coat.

She was about to make a dope deal on foreign territory and didn't have anyone to watch her back. She knew nothing about the cat she was supposed to be meeting besides his name. The shit that Malvo fed her about Stretch being on the up and up went in one ear and out of the other. He may have been cool with customer, but she didn't know jack shit about him. Stretch probably didn't give him any trouble because he was a man with a rep for laying bodies down. The same respect that he extended to Malvo wouldn't necessarily be forwarded to Eureka. Since she was a female he may have looked at her as an easy come-up and try to jack her for the dope. She couldn't take that L. There was too much riding on this exchange to let some sexist asshole come along and screw it up.

"I'm just letting it dry. It should be done in a few minutes," She handed Kenny G the thirty bucks for her ride.

"Baby girl, you in some kind of trouble or something?" he asked concerned as she stuff the three $10 dollar bills into his pocket.

"Nah, I'm Gucci, Pops."

"Look, I don't know what kind of shit you're into but if you're looking to get your hands on some iron, I can make a couple of calls and get something in your hands in under an

60

hour." He glanced at his watch as he twisted the toothpick at the corner of his mouth.

"I'll be alright." She told him. "Besides, my money ain't long enough. Once I pay for this motel room and get something to eat my cash is gonna be a lil' funny."

"You sure?"

She grinned at his concern for her.

"What?" He raised an eyebrow.

"Look at chu, Old head, all worried and shit like you're my father."

"I'm sorry."

"Don't be, it's nice to know that someone cares sometimes," she said with a look of hurt in her eyes. Kenny G moved to comfort her and she shrugged him off. "Don't," she said with attitude. The last thing she wanted to look was vulnerable. She wasn't a weakling and didn't want anyone thinking so. "Alright, I think it's dry." She picked up the cap-gun, wrapped it in the handkerchief and tucked it inside of her jacket.

Once she procured the motel room, she got her bags from out of the trunk of the Buick and said goodbye to him. She tapped the window sill of the driver side door and made to turn around when he grabbed her hand. Turning Eureka's hand palm up, he placed his business card in it and closed it.

"Listen, I don't know how long you're gonna be out here, but if you need a ride again give me a jangle."

"Will do, Pops." Eureka blessed him with her smile and stepped to her motel room's door.

As soon as she crossed the threshold into her room, she locked the door behind her and stripped down. She removed the kilos from her form and laid them out on the bed. She then turned on the A/C to keep the dope cool so it wouldn't go bad. Next, she gathered the bra and panties from her duffle bag and headed to the bathroom.

Fifteen minutes later, she emerged from the bathroom in her bra and panties. After she'd gotten dressed, she placed a call to Stretch to give him the address of the motel she was staying in. She then pulled all of the clothes out of the duffle bag and filled it with nine of the ten kilos. Her eyes took a quick scan of the room until they came across a vent. She retrieved her switch-blade and stepped upon the nightstand. Carefully, she removed the screws that bounded the vent's cover to the wall and tossed it aside. She hoisted up the duffle bag of heroin and pushed it half way inside of the vent.

Eureka was halfway done screwing the vent cover back onto the wall when she heard a knock at the door.

"Who is it?" she called out over her shoulder.

"Stretch."

"Gimmie a sec."

Once Eureka was done with the last screw, she jumped down from off the nightstand and hurriedly straightened up the room. She then tucked the cap-gun into the front of her jeans and took a deep breath. She readied herself and put on her game face. Eureka stole a peek through the peephole. She then unchained and unlocked the door. She opened the door and took in the appearances of her guests before allowing them inside.

Stretch was a tall glass of water that looked like he belonged on the NBA floor. He sported his hair in short twists and had a thin goatee that framed his mouth. He wore gold framed glasses and a thin gold necklace that held to a small crucifix. He was dressed in black silk from head to toe. Beside him was a portly sister with thick calves. She had on a pair of five dollar liquor store shades, a shabby wife beater, and flip flops.

Stretch looked like every bit of those bossed up niggaz out of The Bay that Malvo spoke so highly of. Eureka couldn't put her finger on it, but it was something about him that oozed sophistication. He walked with the air of a Big Willie. From his style and dress you could tell that he was a man of status. It wasn't hard to tell that he was somebody in a world full of nobodies.

"How are you doing, lil' sistah?" Stretch shook her hand. "I'm Stretch and this is my assistant, Fat Fat."

"Reka."

Stretch's eyes shifted down to the cap-gun tucked in the front of Eureka's jeans. He couldn't tell that it was just a toy. It looked authentic to him.

"Smart girl."

"What chu mean?" her face scrunched.

"You brought that heat knowing that you'd be making a transaction with a nigga you don't know from a can of paint. I must commend you. *Trust no man*," he told her. "But next time tote something just a lil' more beefy." He pulled a black, long-nose .44 Magnum revolver from the small of his back and hoisted it up to his shoulder. It was so big that it looked like he had trouble handling it. His wrist looked like it could possibly snap under the weight of the big pistol.

Eureka looked at his big ass revolver unimpressed. She wasn't sure what to feel about him whipping it out on her. She didn't know if he was trying to scare her or what. It really didn't matter because she wasn't so weak that she'd fall apart at the seams.

"What is the point you're tryna get across by pulling out that pistol, Stretch?" she asked. "You tryna intimidate me?"

"Never," he looked insulted that she would even think that. "I'm just tryna give you some sound advice, lil' sistah." Stretch kept it a hundred. "These niggaz in The Bay don't play. So next time you may wanna bring a bigger tool, ya unda dig?" he tucked the .44 Magnum revolver into the small of his back. "Not that you'd have that problem with me. I'm sure Malvo told you that I run a square business."

The Devil Wears Timbs

"Even if you weren't, I ain't studying it," Eureka claimed. "I may be a female, but there ain't a motahfucking thang sweet here. A nigga try me and I'll open his chest up with some heat."

Stretch didn't miss the underlying threat, but he wasn't about to take it there with her.

"Sooooooo," Stretch rubbed his hands together. "You got them joints with you or do you have to go get 'em?"

"They're in a safe place," she answered. "What's up with that paper, though?"

"It's right here." Stretch sat a duffle bag identical to hers on the bed and unzipped it. He held the duffle bag open and allowed Eureka to feast her eyes on the crisp bills stashed inside. Stretch could see she was pleased by the sight before her. "Now tell me how you love that?" he smiled and winked at her.

"That's what I'm talking about, Big baby."

"Lil' sistah, let me get a sample of that product 'fore I set out this bread."

Eureka nodded. She pulled open the dresser drawer and took out the kilo of heroin. She passed it to Stretch and he passed it to Fat Fat. She sat down at the table beside the window and rummaged through her purse. She produced the items she needed to shoot the heroin as well as a vial of green liquid she'd use to test the drugs purity.

Fat Fat cracked opened the kilo of heroin and dipped her long finger nail into it. She scooped up a small pile of the heroin and dumped it into the vial of liquid. As soon as the heroin hit the green liquid it turned blue. She looked to Stretch and they both smiled. From there, Fat Fat went about the task of preparing herself for a shot of the dope. After pulling a tourniquet tight around her arm, she smacked the inside of her forearm until a juicy vein formed. Fat Fat eased the needle into her protruding vein and pushed the poison into her bloodstream. As soon as the dope reached her system she lay

64

back in the chair and closed her eyes. A silly expression formed on her face and she massaged her pussy. If heaven felt like this, she'd welcome death with opened arms.

While all of this was taking place, Eureka was counting up that trap. She was making sure that every dollar was there and accounted for like Malvo told her. She knew how he got down for his and the last thing she needed was a beef with him. It wasn't that she feared him, it was that she already had enough on her plate to deal with. Not to mention she needed that forty grand that this deal would net her.

"Oh yeah, this shit is official." Stretch licked his lips and rubbed his hands together. He couldn't wait to get back to the hood and drop that work on the blocks he had on smash. "Where's the rest of it?"

Eureka took the duffle bag down from the vent and tossed it upon the bed near Stretch. Stretch unzipped the duffle bag and looked the kilos over before zipping it back up.

"That's what I'm talking about, lil' sistah, I like the way you do business."

After the exchange was made, Stretch slapped Fat Fat awake and the two of them made their exit. She locked the door behind them and took a quick peek through the curtains. She then plopped down on the bed and picked up her cell phone. She dialed up Malvo and waited for him to answer. He picked up on the third ring.

"We're A1. I'm on my way back."

She disconnected the call and gathered up her things to take her leave.

Six hours later...

Pow! Pow! Pow! Pow! Bitch, I'm bussin' at 'em/ Ain't no talkin' homie, I'm jus' bussin' at 'em.

The speakers of the Chevy Caprice classic pulsated with Waka Flocka Flame's 'Bustin' at 'em'. Anton sat in the backseat whipping his head from left to right and swinging his

65

arms. He moved swiftly and animatedly, possessed by the music. He was in his own world and no one existed in it beyond him.

Malvo sat behind the wheel nodding his head to the infectious music and taking pulls from a cigarette as he kept a watchful eye out for Eureka. Feeling his cell phone vibrate inside of his pocket, he dipped his meaty hand inside of his jeans and pulled it free. 'Siska' was on the screen. He grumbled and rolled his eyes. He didn't want to answer the call but he knew that it was in his best interest to do so. He turned the stereo down, bringing Anton's animated dancing to a stop.

"What the hell, Malvo?" he frowned. "Why'd you turn it down?"

"Sit cho hyper ass down. I've gotta take this call," Malvo told him before tapping *answer* on the cell phone's screen with his thumb. He placed the cell phone to his ear, conjuring up phony enchantment for the caller.

"Siska, what's happening folks?" he answered jovially.

"Do you have my money?" The caller asked with a no nonsense attitude.

"I'm on it right now. I just need a couple of more days to…" The caller disconnected the call, cutting him short. A worried expressed crossed his face as he looked at the phone as if it was covered in shit.

"Cool. You're off the phone." Anton reached up front to crank the stereo back up and Malvo smacked his hand.

"What's your problem?" He rubbed his stinging hand.

"Don't touch shit in my ride, lil' nigga, you know better." Malvo chastised him like a father would his son.

"I'ma fuck yo fat ass up one day. That's on everything I love, watch." He swore with venom dripping from his vocal cords.

Malvo adjusted the rearview mirror so that he could see into the backseat. Doing so, he met the perturbed eyes of Anton and knew he was as serious as positive HIV results.

"Lil' nigga you need a hundred and fifty pounds and about a foot in height before you're ready to box with The God, you understand me?" Malvo was dead serious.

"I'ma come see about cha when I get my weight up," he swore. "Believe that."

"Well," Malvo mashed out his cigarette in the ashtray. "When you do you make sure you got one of these." He held up his gun so Anton could see it.

"I may be a lil' nigga, but chu gone respect mines," he assured him.

"I hear that slick shit." He turned his attention to the windshield. A smirk appeared on his face when he saw Eureka emerge from the Greyhound station. "Here your sister comes now."

Suddenly, the backseat door flew open and Anton hopped out. He ran over to his sister and hugged her tightly. She hadn't been gone that long, but he missed the hell out of her. The two of them had an unbreakable bond. They were tighter than a G-sting on a five-hundred pound woman. They were brother and sister as well as best friends.

Eureka draped her arm over Anton's shoulders and led him back to the car. Malvo popped the trunk and she dropped the duffle bag inside, slamming it shut. She settled into the front passenger seat and pulled the safety belt across her, buckling it. He wore an ecstatic expression. He was as happy as a pig in shit that she made it back to the city with his trap.

"Alright now, let's get back to the house so I can run up these bands." Malvo fired up the Chevy. He backed out of the parking space and sped out of the parking lot.

The Devil Wears Timbs

Tranay Adams

Chapter 6

Malvo parked the car and everyone hopped out. He snatched the duffle bag from out of the trunk and slammed it shut. He, Eureka and Anton made for the mouth of The Jordan Downs Projects. Loitering out front was a couple of young knuckleheads drinking, blowing down L's and shooting the shit. Silence fell on their conversation once they saw him approaching. They didn't like him much, but they parted like the Red Sea and left a clear path to the black iron-gate that led to the tenements. They may have talked shit about how they would air Malvo out behind his back, but the truth was there was not a soul out of the lot that wanted a problem with him. Everybody and their baby momma knew just how he gave it up. Any funk with him and bullets were going to be exchanged, not words. He didn't play that shit. He was about action and would leave a nigga with a tombstone in a hot minute. Malvo made his way passed the walls of bodies getting nods from some and mad dogs from others.

When Eureka came through the door, she saw Giselle slumped on the couch with her hands nestled in her lap. Drool was running from the corner of her mouth and dripping on her satin gown. She was fast asleep. Eureka saw that the television was still on so she turned it off. She then approached her mother and brushed her hair from out of her face. She leaned closer and kissed her tenderly on the cheek. She grabbed a blanket from out of the top of the hallway closet and draped it over her before continuing into the kitchen.

Malvo dropped the duffle bag at the center of the table. He then searched through the cupboards and the cabinets, growing frustrated with each and every door he opened when he couldn't find what he was looking for. Agitated, he slammed the cabinet's door shut and put his hands on his hips. He brought a meaty palm down his 360 waves as he thought

70

for a second. Recalling something, he snapped his fingers and turned to Anton.

"Anton, get the money-counter outta your mother's bedroom for me," he told him. "It's at the top shelf of the closet, all of the way to the back."

"Why I gotta get it?" Anton asked, holding the fridge open as he looked over its contents.

"'Cause I said so mothafucka," Malvo barked furiously. "So far I'm having an alright day, let's not fuck it up. Okay?"

"Go ahead, Ant," Eureka ruffled his head.

Anton left the kitchen scowling and talking shit under his breath. A moment later, he returned to the kitchen with an old black money-counter. He smacked it down on the table beside the duffle bag and straddled a chair backwards.

"Thank you," Malvo said, but it sounded more like 'Fuck you'.

Malvo reached inside of the duffle bag and grabbed a stack of crispy bills. He popped the rubber-band on the dead faces and dropped them into the counter. He pressed a button on the machine and a green light came on. The machine *beeped* and began shuffling the money. Smiles emerged on Eureka and Anton's faces as they watched the cash flicker through the counter before their eyes. He watched the counter attentively, smiling wickedly and rubbing his hands together.

Once the money-counter finished shuffling through the money, it *beeped* and a red light came on. Malvo organized the money into ten thousand dollars stacks and put rubber-bands around them. He then counted the money by stacks making sure that he had the exact amount he had when he'd ran it through the counter. When that was done he tossed the money into the duffle bag, stack by stack and zipped it closed. He threw the strap of the duffle bag over his shoulder. He was about to make his exit when Eureka spoke out.

"Wait a minute," she called after him. "You're forgetting something."

Lines formed on Malvo's forehead as if he didn't know what the hell she was talking about. "What's that?" he took the time to fire up a cigarette.

Frowning, Eureka looked from Malvo to Anton then back again. *Fuck wrong with this nigga? He ain't that old so I know he's not losing his mind,* she thought.

"My cut," she told him. "The forty racks you promised to give me for making the drop."

"Oh, that? About that," he blew out a cloud of smoke, "I changed my mind. Forty bands is just a lil' too much. I was thinking about giving you, I don't know, say…" his eyes stared off in their corners as he tapped a finger against his chin, thinking. "…nothing!" He burst out laughing like he'd said the funniest shit in the world, but he was the only one laughing. Eureka and Anton weren't amused. "Charge it to the game, lil' momma." He glanced at his titanium Rolex watch and said, "Woo, look at the time. I gotta roll. Y'all take it easy." He ruffled Anton's hair and started for the door.

"Nigga, you got me fucked up!" Eureka darted over to the kitchen sink and grabbed a butcher's knife from out of the pile of wet and dirty dishes. She raced back over to Malvo and slid into the path of the kitchen door, blocking his exit. She held the butcher's knife up, ready to carve his fat ass up like a Christmas goose. "You've got another thing coming if you think you're leaving out this mothafucka without coming up off of mine," she gritted with rage in her eyes and ill intentions in her heart.

"Bitch, you brought a knife to a gun fight?" Malvo barked, spittle flying off his lips. In one swift motion, he snatched the Glock off of his waistline and pointed it at her forehead. Her eyes looked from the gun to his corrupted eyes. She knew that murder had tainted his thoughts and he'd put a hot-one through her brain. But pride was a mothafucka, she wasn't about to let him pull her *ho* card. Her heart pumped Gangster, not bitch. So, if this was going to be the last time she was to drop her nuts and let them hang, then so be it.

While this was going on Anton moved around the kitchen as stealthy as a cat, looking for a weapon to help his sister fend Malvo off with.

"Move the fuck outta my way 'fore I open up your face with some hot shit," Malvo commanded. His teeth were clenched so tight that you could see the skeletal bone structure in his jaws. He'd had *had* it with Eureka. If she didn't move out of his way, then he was going to light her ass up like a Newport.

"I ain't moving nowhere, nigga. You gone have to show me something," she shot back, ready to take a life or have hers taken. It didn't matter because even if she did let him slide she couldn't live the rest of her life knowing that someone had gotten over on her. "You ready to die, nigga?" Eureka seethed.

"You've got some set of balls on you, girl. I hope they'll do you some good where you're going." His eyes penetrated hers as his finger hugged the trigger.

Bloc!

Giselle tackled Malvo and lifted his hand into the air just as the Glock fired, striking the ceiling and causing debris to fall. The two of them fell up against the kitchen sink tussling over the gun. Giselle was putting up one hell of a fight but she was no match for the stronger man. Seeing that she wasn't going to beat him with raw power, Giselle bared her teeth and sunk them into his wrist. He howled in pain and cracked her in the jaw. He then kicked her straight in the chest and sent her sliding across the floor. Malvo moved in on her to finish her off. He went to level his Glock between her eyes and a growl came from his rear. He was just about to turn around when he felt a small body slam against his back. Then there was the blood curdling scream when he felt steak knives being jammed into each of his shoulders. Malvo spun around in circles trying to yank Anton off of his back. When he couldn't reach him he kicked off of the kitchen counter. The weight of his body came down upon Anton's body and knocked the wind from out of him.

During the melee, Eureka scrambled to find the Glock. She knew Anton didn't stand a snow ball's chance in hell against him. He was in so much pain from Malvo falling on top of him that he couldn't put up much of a fight. Malvo clenched his teeth and threw his head back against Anton's mouth, busting his grill and bloodying his teeth.

Anton lay on the floor cupping his bloody mouth with both hands. Malvo slowly got to his feet and pulled the steak knives from out of his shoulders. He dropped the crimson stained knives to the floor and scanned the kitchen.

"Looking for this?" A voice came from Malvo's rear. He spun around and found Eureka pointing his piece at him.

"What're you gonna do with that?" Malvo asked with menacing eyes and a heaving chest. Blood ran from the wounds in his shoulders and down his arms, dripping onto the floor. "You aren't built for no bodies. I bet cha don't even have the stones to pull the…"

Bloc!

A bullet skinned Malvo's cheek and a sliver of blood ran down. His eyes were as wide as saucers and his mouth hung open. He touched his cheek and his fingers came away with blood. He mad dogged Eureka and clenched his jaws.

"You lil' four foot skeeza. I'm gonna take that gun and fuck you with it." Malvo lunged at Eureka and a bullet struck him in the shoulder, dropping him to a knee.

She pointed the weapon at his dome and rested her finger on the trigger, sneering she said, "Lights out, cock…"

Malvo swung his duffle bag at Eureka's hand and it swung aside, firing the Glock. A hole appeared on the wall. He jumped to his feet and kicked her in the chest, slamming her up against the refrigerator. He then bolted for the front door. Eureka snatched up the gun and went after him. When she reached the kitchen doorway he was disappearing through the front door. She pursued him outside where he hauled ass, holding his bleeding shoulder. The residents of The Jordan Downs scattered getting the fuck up out of the way but staying close enough to watch what was about to happen. Eureka was so furious that she didn't even notice them. She was so focused on taking Malvo off of his feet that only she and he existed.

Malvo reached the driver's door of his Chevy. He stuck the key into its lock. He was about to turn it when the window exploded and sent broken glass raining on the ground. He kept it moving, running as fast as he could with the five foot five gunner hot on his trail.

"Ol' hoe ass nigga. You thought shit was candy here?" Eureka growled angrily, aiming that Glock at his back as he ran, sprinkling the asphalt with his blood.

"Rekkkka!" Anton bellowed at her rear, standing beside their mother.

Bloc!

A heat rock whizzed by Malvo's ear and nearly severed it. The threat of the bullet being so close cranked up his heart rate. He could literally feel it slamming up against the interior of his left peck. He darted out into the street, whipping around after being blinded by headlights. His eyes bulged and mouth dropped open, but before he could release a scream he went flying over the hood of a Mazda. All of the money from the duffle bag went up into the air, and came back down, slapping against the asphalt. The sight of that much dough sent the residents of The Jordan Downs projects and the few people out in the street into pandemonium. A wave of people collided into the street, snatching as much money as they could. Even the driver of the Mazda hopped out to snatch a couple of dollars.

Anton and Giselle ran out into the street trying to salvage as much of the money as they could too. Eureka, still in kill-mode, gripping the gat with both hands, moved in to write the last chapter of Malvo's life. She entered the anxious flock of vultures kicking them aside and threatening them with her weapon. When the crowd dispersed, Malvo was gone. The only thing on the ground was blood stains.

"Shit! Shit! Shit!" She fumed and swung at the air in despair, wishing Malvo was right there to receive his punishment. She whipped around to find them stuffing their pockets with the last of the money on the ground. "We've gotta get back into the house, come on." She pulled Giselle by the wrist toward the house and Anton followed.

Eureka slammed the door shut, locking and chaining it. Motioning with the heat in her hand, she told Anton and Giselle to count up the money they'd recovered. While mother and son did as they were instructed, Eureka glanced out of the curtains and saw two police cruisers pulling into the projects. Their red and blue lights shined in through the window upon her face.

When the police hopped out of their cruisers asking questions, Mr. Rifkins emerged from a crowd of onlookers and engaged them. Eureka pulled her head back from the window and darted into the kitchen. She grabbed the dish towel from off of the sink and wiped her prints off of the heater. She then wrapped it up in tinfoil and stuck it at the back of the freezer, camouflaging it amongst the few frozen meats that were inside. She then ducked back off into the living room where Anton and Giselle were counting up the money.

"How much are we working with?" Eureka inquired.

"Two racks," Anton reported.

"Boy, learn how to count, its fifteen hundred dollars here." Giselle tossed the money she'd counted on the coffee table.

"What?" Creases formed on Anton's forehead as he looked at Giselle like she'd lost her wig. "It was two racks here." He snatched up her money and put it with his, recounting it. He looked to Eureka and shook his head. "Nuh uh, mommy's living foul. There was just two racks here, sis."

"Mommy, come up off that." She motioned with her hand.

"I ain't got nothing, baby. I swear to God." Giselle swore, hands up in the air, looking innocent than a mothafucka.

"I must look like Boo Boo the Fool to you." She approached her mother. "Stand up." Giselle stood up from the sofa with her hands up. She rolled her eyes as Eureka gave her a thorough pat down. Irritated, she exhaled and gave her the side eye like she knew that she was guilty.

"See, I told you I didn't have nothing." Giselle sat back down on the sofa.

"Uh huh," Eureka said. She wasn't buying that bullshit that her mother was trying to sell. "Strip down to your underwear, ma."

"Girl, bye," Giselle waved her off as she picked up her pack of smokes. "I'm *your* momma, you aren't mine. You better gone somewhere with that. I told you that I didn't have nothing." She fired up a Joe and lay back on the sofa, blowing smoke.

Eureka was about to press her mother but knocks at the door stopped her.

"See if that's The Boys, Ant." She whispered to her brother, throwing her head toward the front door.

Anton nodded and obliged his sister, taking a glance through the peephole.

"I gotta use the bathroom." Giselle hopped up from the couch and heading toward the bathroom.

"It's Mr. Rifkins," he announced.

"Let 'em in."

77

Anton unchained and unlocked the door. He pulled the door open and allowed Mr. Rifkins inside. He exchanged pleasantries with them before removing his cap.

"What's up?" Eureka folded her arms across her chest.

"Well, the police are gone."

"What's that supposed to mean to me?"

A smirk emerged on Mr. Rifkins' face. He looked down at his shoes and then back up at Eureka. "You don't have to worry about nothing. No one's saying anything; The Jordan's protect their own."

"That's what's up," she replied.

"Well," Mr. Rifkins cleared his throat and slapped his cap back upon his head. "I guess I'll be going about my business."

"Alright." Eureka showed him to the door.

When she opened the door, he grabbed it and quietly closed it shut. "Okay, that's enough of the bullshit." Mr. Rifkins began, shedding the skin of the humble old man that the projects were used to. "You need to take your family and get the fuck outta these projects tonight. Malvo is a dangerous, dangerous man. If I know him, he'll be back here in the next couple of days with a hit squad to exterminate every living, breathing soul in this unit. If you've never listened to me before, for God's sake listen to me now. Pack up and get the hell outta dodge. If you want I'll drive you myself, but you need to leave tonight!"

Eureka held Mr. Rifkins gaze for a moment. Time and space seemed to have grown still as she gave what he'd said some serious thought. She nodded and he sighed with relief that she was going to do the smart thing and get from out of The Bricks while she still could.

"Good," Mr. Rifkins said. "Listen, I'm gonna go up to my place and grab my keys. I'll be back here in ten minutes, be ready."

Eureka nodded and closed the door shut, locking it.

"Where are we going to go?"

"I don't know yet. But he's right we've gotta get ghost," she said. "Malvo and his boys are most definitely gonna roll back."

"Right."

"Pack us up a few things," she commanded. "I'll whip us up a couple of lunches."

"Okay." Anton started for their bedroom but turned around, brow furrowed. "Where did mommy go?"

"Bathroom," Eureka answered. She engaged the bathroom door and pounded on it with a fist. "Ma, come on out. We've gotta get out here." When there wasn't an answer, she pounded on the door again, calling for her to come out. Eureka left the door and returned with a butter knife. Gripping the door knob tightly, she jimmied the lock with the butter knife until it popped open. When she and Anton stepped inside, the bathroom window was open and Giselle was gone.

Chapter 7

Malvo winced as he looked at his wounded arm which was now in a sling. When he'd gotten hit by that Mazda he thought for sure that he was a goner. His arm was inflamed and his back was screaming at him. He could barely manage to move, and believed that God had finally called his number. He just knew that at any moment Eureka was going to come running up to finish him off. Fortunately, the saying that *God watches over fools and babies* was true.

The spill of all of that money ignited a riot in the middle of the street. The surge of people created a diversion that he used to his advantage. He ran down the block and hid under the porch of a nearby house. Once the police presence had died down, he hailed a cab to King Drew Hospital. He walked through the emergency ward's doors as if he hadn't gotten blasted an hour ago. He was so cool and calm when he told the nurse at the front desk he'd been shot that she thought he was joshing. It wasn't until he showed her the hole in his arm that she'd taken him seriously. Malvo was rushed into the back room where a doctor took stock of the damage the bullet had done. The projectile had gone straight through his arm missing his brachial artery by a hair. He had been lucky because if that artery would have been severed he'd be lying face up in a coffin with a pastor reciting his eulogy.

Fucking Eureka! When I catch up with that skeeza, I'm gonna jam a spiked bat up her cunt, he thought. *I'm the wrong one to fuck with. I don't play that shit.*

The pain killers that Malvo was given had begun to wear off and he started to feel the aching of his arm. The doctor told him that he'd have the nurse bring him a couple of more pills but that was twenty minutes ago and he needed something to relieve the pain now. Fishing inside of the pockets of his leather jacket, he produced a pre-rolled joint.

He smiled devilishly as he dragged the blunt under his nose, inhaling it. He moved to head into the restroom to sneak a couple of tokes when he heard someone approaching. He snatched the joint from out of his mouth and stashed it inside of his sling just as a pretty nurse entered the room with two small paper cups, one containing water and the other containing two pain pills.

"How are you doing there, gorgeous?" Malvo flashed his sexiest smile as he massaged his chin, so that she could see that huge icy gold pinky ring of his. He looked her up and down, licking his lips like he was thirsty for her.

"I'm fine." She smiled back, causing her cheeks to dimple as she passed him his medicine and water.

"Oh, I can see that," he capped, taking the cups. She blushed and giggled falling for his weak ass advances. Malvo tossed the pain killers back and washed them down with the water. Thanking the nurse, he crushed the two paper cups and tossed them into the waste basket. She told him that the doctor would be in shortly to see him before turning to leave. *Lord have mercy,* he thought watching the nurse's big bodacious ass swing from left to right as she disappeared through the doorway.

Malvo straightened up when the doctor stepped into the room. They exchanged pleasantries. He listened to the doctor tell him about the antibiotics and the pain killer medications he'd written on the prescription slips.

Once Malvo had gotten a clear understanding of his medications, they shook hands and the doctor took his leave. He hung his leather jacket on the shoulder of his injured arm, tucked the prescripts slips into his pocket and started for the door. He got about five feet from the threshold when two uniform cops emerged, one, a tall white stud with a superhero's physique and ponytail. The other an Amazon with long brunette hair, pulled back in a bun. They were both Caucasian and wore hostile expressions.

Malvo rolled his eyes and sighed. He damn sure wasn't up for dealing with their bullshit.

"Look, bruh," Malvo began. "I'ma tell y'all like I told your homies. I don't know sh…" that was as far as he got before Ponytail punched him square in the mouth. He staggered back, bumping into the hospital bed and hitting the linoleum. He eyes blinked like he didn't know what had hit him and he touched his bloody lip. He looked up to see the Amazon locking the door while ponytail snatched him up to his feet.

"Where's the money?" Ponytail asked through clenched teeth.

"I don't have it right now but…"

"Wrong answer!" Ponytail gave him a three punch combination that dropped him to his knees, gasping for air and hugging his stomach. The Amazon stood by the door with her arms folded across her chest watching him get his ass beat. Ponytail dog walked Malvo over to the rest room. He snatched the door open, flipped on the light switch and kicked up the commode's lid. The commode's water was discolored yellow from him pissing in it earlier and not flushing it.

"Wait! Wait! I…" Malvo's head was sent plunging deep inside of the toilet bowl. His arm flailed wildly and his legs thrashed around as he tried to get away. A film of sweat formed on Ponytail's forehead and a sinister smile graced his lips as he held Malvo's head down in the water. When he yanked his head back, he belched and spat out the piss water.

Before a discombobulated Malvo could say another word, his head was dunk back inside of the toilet bowl. Ponytail held him there for a time before yanking his head back up. He gulped in air and that nasty ass water dripped from off of his face. Ponytail released him and went for his waistline. Malvo went to rush him but the Amazon drawing her weapon on him slowed his roll.

Ponytail pulled out a cell phone and speed dialed a number. He put the cell phone on speaker and held it up as it rang. On the fifth ring an older distinguished man picked up. The older man didn't wait for the caller to give him an introduction. He went on to speak with a voice that led you to believe that he was suffering from a bad cold.

"Malvo, I take it that you don't have my money. Would I be correct in assuming this?"

"Look, man, I don't have the money yet, but give me a lil' more time to piece some things together and I promise I'll come through with that."

For a time the older man didn't say a word, but then he broke his silence.

"That man that you murdered was the sole provider of his family. With him gone his wife and kids will be left to fend for themselves. Seeing as how he worked for me, and was one damn good earner, I promised his wife half of a million dollars as workman's compensation. Now, that money was supposed to have come from you, like we agreed. But since you haven't anted up as of late I took it upon myself to give his wife the money out of my own pocket. Now, you're indebted to me."

Two weeks ago, Malvo got into a dispute over a parking space outside of a night club. He'd stolen a parking space that someone had clearly been waiting on. The driver of the other car hopped out of his vehicle popping shit and demanding that he move his car. Malvo flipped the dude off and proceeded to open the passenger door for his wife. He was helping her slip on her mink coat when the irate driver kicked his car and spit on its hood. Pissed off, Malvo popped the trunk of his ride and grabbed a tire iron. He ran up behind the irate man and cracked him in the back of the skull. He hit the ground and his body went through convulsions, shaking violently as he went into shock. Malvo and his wife hopped back into his ride and got the fuck out of dodge. Unbeknownst to them, the driver's wife was slumped down into the passenger seat peering just over the dashboard, watching the whole scenario unfold. She'd made a mental description of Malvo and the license plate of his car. She reported this information to her husband's boss who just so happened to be the head honcho of an infamous crime syndicate.

After tracking Malvo down, the boss sent a host of his men to pay him a visit. They snatched him out of his house while he was still in his boxers and brought him before their boss. The boss drew a barber's razor and was about to slit his throat from ear to ear until he begged and pleaded for his life. The boss took pity on Malvo and allowed him to live. He placed an offer on the table. *Your life in exchange for five hundred thousand dollars.* Without a second thought, Malvo agreed to the deal and was set free.

That was two weeks ago. Now it was time to make good on the agreement.

"Look, I got like fifty stacks. I can hit chu off with that until I get the rest together."

"How long?"

"I just got to run to the house and ..."

"No, how long before you get the $500 thousand dollars?"

"Two, three months, maybe."

"No. You have one more week, my friend."

"One week?" Malvo asked like it wasn't enough time.

"Kill 'em!"

The Amazon pointed her heater between Malvo's eyes.

"No! No! No!" He raised his hand. "A week is good. A week is fine. I'll have it then."

"Good," The older man said. "If you try to renege and run, I will find you and skin you alive. Do I make myself clear?"

"You got it."

"Very well then."

Ponytail took the cell phone off of speaker and brought it to his ear. He listened to what the old man had to say and then hung up. He stared at Malvo for a while before turning on his heels and following the Amazon out of the room. He sighed with relief and laid his head back against the tiled wall. It had been one hell of a night.

*****

"I'll explain everything when I get there." Malvo spoke into his cell phone as he emerged from the double electric doors of the emergency ward, making a beeline toward the black on black Escalade truck idling at the curb. "Calm the fuck down. Everything is gonna be fine, okay? You just make sure you have you and Heaven's shit packed when I get there. I just wanna pull in and pull out when I arrive. I love you too. See you in a minute." He disconnected the call and slid into the backseat of the truck, slamming the door shut.

"What the fuck?" Crunch's nose wrinkled smelling the repugnant odor expelling from Malvo. He pulled his shirt over his nose to conceal it from the aroma. Crunch was a six foot nigga with skin the color of 12 o'clock midnight. He wore several cheap gold chains and you could almost always spot him rocking a sweat suit.

"Goddamn, Mal. Smells like you've been marinating in piss," Ronny declared, pinching his nose closed. He was a skinny bronze complexioned dude with a head shaped like a light bulb. He sported a shaved head, a nose like Scotty Pipen and elf like ears.

"Let me crack a window in this mothafucka," Crunch held down the buttons that descended the SUV's windows. A cool wind blew in and dissipated the overwhelming smell of urine.

"You bring that burner with you?" Malvo asked Crunch.

85

"Yeah," Crunch replied as he threw the Escalade in drive and drove off.

"Ronny, look in the glove-box and give 'em that strap."

Ronny did as he was told. When Malvo took the burner, he ejected the magazine and made sure that it was fully loaded. He then smacked that hoe back in and slapped one into its chamber.

"So, Boss Dog, you gone let us know what happened up there?" Crunch asked.

Crunch jumped on the 405 freeway heading toward Santa Monica. He and Ronny listened to Malvo relay to them what had gone down back at the hospital. After hearing how they had played their man, they were ready to find the opposition and put some iron to them.

"I say we find these niggaz tonight and throw 'em a going away party," Ronny said.

"You read my mind, Ronny. You know a nigga breathe for the bullshit," Crunch conceded.

"Normally, I would give y'all the nod on a violation like this but I gotta ask y'all to fallback," Malvo said, garnering his goons' grimaces. They couldn't believe that he wanted them to put their bangers on the shelves. This was odd to them because Malvo loved to beef like he loved to breathe.

"Fuck you talking about?" The lines in Crunch's forehead deepened. "These niggaz violated you, dawg. Straight up disrespected you. We've gotta answer back and we've gotta answer back now!" His fist slammed against the steering wheel.

"You two niggaz are always ready to do some shit, man," Malvo replied. "Chill the fuck out and think sometimes. I don't have enough funds or enough guns to lock horns with this bull. My best bet is to try to run these bands up and break this mothafucka off. If I can't make his quota, then we get on our gangsta tip, alright?" He looked from Crunch to Ronny as he sat in the backseat. He could tell that they weren't feeling him or his argument but he hoped that they'd go along with what he had planned.

"Alright, fam," Crunch agreed to go along.

Malvo looked to Ronny. "What's up, Ron Ron? You still down for me, big dawg?"

"Shit, you gave a nigga a shot when no one else would. I'ma ride with you 'til the wheels fall off," Ronny assured.

"That's what I'm talking about. Y'all my mothafucking niggaz," Malvo pulled the joint from out of his leather jacket and sparked it up.

"Now, gimmie the rundown on this lil' bitch from The Jordan Downs," Crunch said.

Malvo took two deep pulls from the joint and passed it up front to his goons. He then went on to tell them about what went down between he and Eureka. By the time he had finished telling his story, they were pulling up to his crib out in Westwood. Malvo told his goons to keep their eyes and ears open as he slid out of the truck to get his wife and kid. When he opened the door of his house he found his twenty year old wife, Faith, and their five year old daughter, Heaven, sitting on the sofa, three suitcases sat off to the side.

"Daddy," Heaven sang, hopping from her mother's lap and ran over to her father. Malvo quickly scooped her up with his good arm and kissed her chubby cheeks. Little Heaven was a red skinned cutie with grayish brown hair and hazel green eyes. She was the exact replica of her mother, only smaller.

"Eww, you stink, Daddy. You need a bath," her nose scrunched up. "And what happened to your arm and shoulders?" her little forehead crinkled as she looked upon her father with concern.

"Me and your uncle Crunch and Ron Ron were playing around and I got hurt," Malvo told her. "But don't worry, baby. This isn't nothing a couple of those famous kisses of your can't fix." That brought a big smile to Heaven's face. Her

87

tiny hands cupped her father's face and she kissed his lips twice.

"Malvo, what happened out there?" Faith asked as she approached him.

He looked at the luggage and noticed that there weren't any toys alongside it for his daughter to play with. He turned to Heaven and said, "Baby, why don't you go find you a couple of toys to play with? You're gonna need something to do on your way out to Rancho Cucamonga to your grand parents' house."

"Okay, Daddy," Heaven dashed out of the living room and into her bedroom.

"Rancho Cucamonga?" Faith raised an eyebrow. "What's happened that makes you think that we'll be safer at my parents' house?"

Malvo gave her a look and that's all she needed to know to understand what he was talking about. "Oh, my God. I thought you had the money to pay those people off," she held her hand to her heart. She was scared. Faith knew the cats that he had gotten tangled up with were bad men, very bad men.

Siska, their boss, that nigga had reach. It didn't matter where you were in the world, he would find your mothafuckin' ass. Him and the rest of those suit and tie rocking gangsters made the studs in The Godfather movie look like a couple of Care Bears. They earned the right to be written on the 'Do Not Fuck with These Niggaz' list.

"I did have it. The drop was as smooth as a baby's ass, but that hood rat Eureka fucked it up," he vented, snarling and swinging on the air with his good arm.

"Who is Eureka and what did she do?"

"The bitch I got to make the drop, baby," Malvo told her. "She shot me then ran off with the money I was going to use to pay off these people with." As quickly as the lie formed in his head, it rolled off of his tongue.

"See, that's why I told you to let me do it," Faith said, with her hands on her hips.

"Did you really think that I was going to put the mother of my daughter in jeopardy? Fuck that! She provided a service and I paid her for it," he shook his head and ran a hand down his face. "Everything was kosher until this bitch got greedy."

"It's okay, baby. Everything is going to be alright." Faith kissed him on the cheek and stroked the side of his face.

"You better believe it is," Malvo swore. "'Cause I'ma crush her lil' thieving ass."

"I know you are, boo, 'cause you're my man and you can do anything you put your mind to."

He pulled Faith into him and kissed her hard and sensually.

"Ewww, I don't wanna see dat," Heaven returned to the living room with two Brat dolls. Her words interrupted her parents making out. They both turned to her wiping the extra spit from their lips.

"Faith, take Heaven and get into the truck. I'll be out in the minute," Malvo told her. On second thought, he pulled out his cell phone and scrolled through his contacts. "Matter of fact, fall back, I'ma have Crunch and Ronny help you bring this stuff out to his truck."

While Crunch and Ronny busied themselves helping Faith with the luggage, Malvo ducked off into the bedroom and into the closet. He pulled the string and restored light to dark area. He then peeled back a patch of the carpet and exposed a black digital safe. He punched in the combination to the safe. It beeped and the door popped open. He grabbed every stack of money that was inside of the safe and tossed it into a pillowcase. He put everything back in place and closed the closet door on his way out.

Malvo slid into the backseat of the Escalade truck and sat the pillowcase down on the floor between his legs. Faith snuggled up beside him and closed her eyes while Heaven lay across his lap and closed her eyes. He kissed them both on their heads and laid his head back against the headrest. As soon as he got back from dropping his family off in Rancho Cucamonga, Malvo was going to take it back to The Jordan Downs projects and smoke everybody in Eureka's apartment. He closed his eyes and a smile stretched across his face. He drifted off as the Escalade coasted through the streets. His dreams were about the many ways he saw himself killing Eureka and her family.

Chapter 8

Eureka and Anton sat on the sofa in the living room with their bags packed waiting on Mr. Rifkins to return. Giselle running off was confirmation that she'd stolen some of the money. She didn't have to rack her brain wondering where her mother had gone. Since she had money in her pocket, Eureka knew that she was going somewhere to get high, and she knew just the place.

Knocks at the door snatched them from their thoughts. Eureka gave Anton the signal to fall back as she drew her Glock, stepping to the front door cautiously and taking a gander through the peephole. Seeing that it was Mr. Rifkins, she tucked the iron into the small of her back and undid the locks. When she opened the door, she found him wearing a fedora and a trench coat. She looked down to his side and he was gripping a shotgun threw his trench coat pocket.

"Y'all ready?" he asked.

"Yeah, but I'm gonna need you to take me to get my mother."

"Bugsy's spot?" Eureka nodded sadly. "Alright, let's get outta here."

He pulled his Toyota pickup truck to a two story house on 105th and Juniper. Eureka looked up at the big raggedy house that looked like a horror movie could be filmed on its premises. She'd been here a gazillion times before to find her mother so that she could get her EBT card to get groceries and the rent money off of it before she could spend it all. She had gotten so familiar with the fiends there that she knew them all by name.

"Stay here, Ant. I'll be right back."

"Alright."

Eureka hopped out of the Toyota pickup truck and hustled up the steps of the condemned house. She knocked in a distinct pattern, waited a few moments and then knocked one last time. She waited a couple of minutes and then raised her fist to knock again. Her knuckles were about to touch the door when she heard the locks coming undid. The door swung open and a man of a stocky build stood before her. He was a youthful looking cat about twenty-five to twenty-eight years old. A black snapback with a purple 'W' sat cocked to the side on his dome. The crisp purple Dickies suit he sported looked like it was having trouble containing his bulging muscles. One hand brought the roach of the blunt to his lips while the other held tightly to a Tec-9. His eyes were shifty like he was expecting for some shit to go down at any moment. This mammoth of a man didn't need an introduction because his name was on the tongues of every dope fiend in the neighborhood. He had some of the best dope east of Watts. His product was sweet. It kept his pockets lined and his dick wet.

"Watts up, Bugsy?"

"Watts up, Reka?"

"Ain't shit, my mom here?"

Bugsy took one last pull of the roach and flicked it aside. His head whipped from left to right making sure there wasn't anybody watching him.

"Yeah, come on." He waved her in with the Tec-9.

Bugsy closed the door behind Eureka once she stepped inside of the house. She watched as he chained the door, locked about six locks, and pulled a metal slab across it. He then used a key to lock about three more locks before stashing it into his pocket.

Walking past Eureka, he tapped her arm and motioned for her to follow him. She followed behind Bugsy as he led the way. She took in the full scope of the two storied, six bedroom house. All of the walls had been knocked down so there was nothing but wall to wall hardwood floor.

Her face twisted with disgust. She gagged when the overwhelming odor of blood, piss and feces assaulted her sense of smell. No matter how many times she came into contact with that scent she'd never get used to it. She didn't understand how anyone could. Eureka pulled her shirt over the lower half of her face and continued her trek through the house.

With each step she took she heard crunching beneath her sneakers. That's when she noticed that the floor was covered in loose trash and drug paraphernalia. She took a gander at all of the people scattered throughout the house. They were shooting dope, preparing to shoot dope, or shooting dope into someone else's arm for them.

Eureka even saw a couple of D-boys she knew from around the way in there. One was standing off in the corner with his head tilted back against the wall. He held one hand behind his back while the other held the neck of the white chick down on her knees before him. Her long blonde hair slightly bounced as her mouth moved up and down his dick with rapid speed. From the look on the D-boy's face she could tell that he was about ready to cum.

"Yeah, bitch, a nigga told you he was gone fuck the dog shit out chu!" Another D-boy's voice came from Eureka's left. She looked to find a chunky woman with short nappy hair down on all fours on a filthy mattress. Her big long, floppy breasts swung back and forth as the scrawny D-boy slammed his pelvis into her meaty behind. Each pump caused a ripple to travel up the woman's buttocks.

"Ah, fuck, I'm cuming, I'm cuming, cuz." The D-boy clenched his jaws and bared his bunched teeth. Three more pumps and he jumped to his feet, clutching his glistening dick. He stepped to the front of the chunky woman and held her face up. With a grunt, he bust on her mouth and rubbed his dick-head back and forth across her lips. The D-boy took the time to admire his handiwork then his head snapped in her direction. His eyes narrowed and his lips twisted.

"Fuck you looking at?"

Eureka turned back around to catch up with Bugsy. When she reached him he was standing at the foot of the staircase.

"She's upstairs in the bathroom. It's down the hall and to ya right," Bugsy motioned with his hand. "I'ma post up right here and wait for you."

"Okay, thanks," she said before going up the staircase.

When Eureka entered the bathroom she found Giselle slumped in the grimy bathtub. She had drawn up a shot of heroin and had brought it to the thick vein in her arm.

"Mommy?" her eyes flooded with tears and obscured her vision. Her bottom lip quivered uncontrollably and her skin felt hot as her heart thumped inside of her chest. The pain she felt seeing her mother about to shoot up dope was indescribable. She couldn't begin to form the words for someone to understand how she felt at that moment. But if she had to give someone an idea she would have to say that it was comparable to a searing spear piercing her sternum.

Although, she had seen her mother like this a billion times, Eureka could never grow accustomed to it. She couldn't understand that if her mother loved her and Anton as much as she claimed she did why she couldn't just quit cold turkey. She believed wholeheartedly that her mother loved dope more than she loved them. In one hand, she had dope and in the other she had her children. If she were to subtract the one that meant the least to her, then she should end up with the one she loved the most, her children. The shit was multiplication not trigonometry. Though it had been explained to her that it wasn't her mother but the drug that was in control, Eureka didn't believe that. She believed in the phrase '*Love conquers all'*. Therefore, her mother's love for them should have won over her addiction to dope.

She turned her back on her mother and wiped her tears with the back of her hand. She then took the time to gather herself before turning around and reentering the bathroom.

"Mommy," she called her mother a second time.

"Debbie, this must be some good dope if it got chu seeing ya momma and shit." Giselle said, thinking that her get-high buddy was still in the bathroom with her. "May ass has been dead for the past twenty years."

Feeling the tears trying to resurface, Eureka closed her eyes and took deep breaths. Once her breathing was under control, she opened her eyes and sat down on the edge of the bathtub.

"Mommy, it's me. Eureka."

Giselle lazily looked up at her through hooded eyes. An easy smile stretched across her face.

"Hey, Reka, how's momma's oldest baby?"

"I'm fine."

"Come on, I got us a ride." She went to rise from the edge of the bathtub but what Giselle said next stalled her.

"I'm not going."

"What do you mean you aren't going?" Eureka frowned.

Giselle pierced the thick vein with her needle and pushed the poison into her bloodstream. As soon as the drug entered her body, it began to work its magic. Giselle closed her eyes and licked her chapped lips as she lay back in the bathtub.

"Mommy, what do you mean?"

"Reka, let's face it, baby. Your momma ain't worth a damn," Giselle spoke truthfully of herself. "You and Ant will do better without me out there."

"No, that's not true," Eureka quickly reprimanded. She looked at defeat swim in Giselle's eyes as her mother's lips trembled from the pain of the truthful words she spoke.

"It—is, baby," Giselle's speech slurred as the effect of the high evolved.

Eureka grimaced as she looked at the decrepit bathroom she was in, petitioning for her mother to come home, wherever that was.

"Pleeeeease—" Giselle words trailed. "With me coming along you'll have —two kids instead of one."

Eureka could feel the warmth in her eyes, which meant the tears wasn't far behind.

"I'll—I'll—I'll crash at Debs for the time being. Trust me— you'll be alright. You—you just get a decent job—look after your brother. You'll see, baby, everything—everything—everything will work its self out."

"Well, what about Anton? He's only fifteen. He still needs his mother," she tried her best to reason.

"Fifteen—fifteen—" Giselle fought to stay afloat. "That's a grown man in this neighborhood. You know that, Reka. Anton needs me—me about as much as I need a dick growing outta the side of my—head."

Eureka swallowed her spit and fought back the tears that were sure to come.

"Me, you, Ant, we're all we got, ma. We're family. A broken one, but a family still." Her voice cracked feeling the raw emotion overpowering her will to keep it at bay.

"There—there is no me in that—in that picture, baby. Ya momma's been as good as dead since—since your father's passing." Hot tears slicked her cheeks. She cleared her throat and tried to find a more comfortable position inside of the bathtub.

Eureka's face scrunched up and lines formed across her nose as she stared at her mother nodding off inside of the bathtub. The tears seemed to slide down her cheeks one after another, rapidly. Her top lip twitched with anger and she felt what she could only describe as a ball of fire forming in the pit of her stomach.

"No! No! No!" She grabbed her by the wrist and started pulling on her arm, trying to get her up out of the bathtub. "Get up, it's time to go! I'm sick of having to take responsibility. I'm sick of having to carry the burden on my shoulders! It's not fair, it's not fair!" she pulled and pulled on Giselle's arm, but she wouldn't budge. She was dead weight sitting inside of the bathtub. Slowly, the seams on the shoulder of her jean jacket began to split until finally they came loose and she fell back, holding the sleeve of her mother's jacket.

Eureka lay on her back on the scummy floor clutching both sides of her head as she sobbed long and hard. She made a hideous face as the tears flowed like rain sliding down glass, rolling off the sides of her face and dripping onto the floor. Snot began to form inside of her nose and peek out the rim of her nostrils. "It's not fair, it's not fair, it's fair!" She kept on repeating.

It wasn't fair that her father had been murdered. It wasn't fair that her mother had gotten strung out on heroin. It wasn't fair that she was forced to take up the responsibility of running a household at such a young age. It wasn't fair that they were so poor and lived in a shitty apartment in the projects.

Eureka Jackson was absolutely right. It wasn't fair, but it was life, her life and she had to make the best out of it. Once she came down from sobbing, she lay on her back staring up at the ceiling. She then closed her eyes and opened them, wiping her face of the tears. Getting up to her knees, she crawled over to the bathtub. She took a hold of Giselle's hand, kissing it and then her forehead. She picked herself up and walked to the door. Before she crossed the threshold, she turned back around to her mother.

The Devil Wears Timbs

"I guess this is goodbye then," Eureka said. "I love you, mommy."

With that being said, she kissed her palm and blew her mother a kiss, before disappearing through the doorway.

Eureka left the shooting gallery with a heavy head and an even heavier heart. The Toyota pickup truck was parked directly across the street, but it seemed like it was a thousand miles away. Her ankles felt like they were shackled to boulders with each step that she took. She didn't know what to say to Anton when he asked about their mother. She knew that she couldn't tell him that she'd abandoned them because that would break his heart more than her death would. She wanted to tell him that she died of a drug overdose and had been taken away. But she knew that if he was to ever find out that she'd lied to him, he'd never speak to her again.

Eureka hopped into the pickup truck and slammed the door shut. Anton looked to her with a creased forehead wondering where their mother was. A few moments had passed before he asked of her whereabouts, but that was as long as Eureka needed to decide whether she was going to tell a lie or the truth.

"Reka, where's mommy?"

"Let's go, Mr. Rifkins," she said then looked to Anton. "She didn't want to come along, Ant. It's just me and you now," her voice cracked with emotion and a single tear descended her cheek. "We're all we got," her bottom lip quivered.

Anton wiped his sister's tear away with his thumb and interlocked his fingers with hers. "We're all we need, sis. We're all we need," he kissed her hand.

He laid his head against her shoulder as the Toyota pickup truck coasted through the streets.

"Where are we headed now?" Mr. Rifkins asked.

"To the cheapest motel you can find." Eureka stared out of the passenger side window. She then laid her head

against Anton's, allowing her thoughts to take her away from her harsh reality.

Chapter 9
Seventeen minutes later they arrived.

"We're here," Mr. Rifkins looked to Eureka who sat up looking around.

"What's the name of this place?" she inquired.

"The Snooty Fox," he replied.

"*The Snooty Fox?*" Anton took a gander at the motel and was surprised by its exceptional appearance. Given the neighborhood it was in, he was expecting it to be the grandfather of all shitholes. "This place doesn't look half bad," he smirked.

"It's kind of nice," Eureka agreed. She turned to Mr. Rifkins. "You sure this place is cheap?"

"Yep, I've been here a number of times." He removed his glasses and cleaned its lenses with a rag. "The place is dirt cheap and modestly decorated. If you want to down grade even further, I could take you to this joint out in Compton. Its thirty bucks a night there, but if you want my advice, crash here. It's a cool lil' spot to lay ya head."

"I can imagine how that dump must look." Eureka envisioned the motel out in Compton. "Let me see how much this place is going to run me."

A few minutes later she returned to the pickup truck. He let down his window.

"I got us a week," Eureka announced. "Come on, Ant," she motioned for her baby brother to get out of the truck. Anton grabbed the rest of their things and hopped out of the truck. He went to stand beside his sister outside of Mr. Rifkins' window.

"Thanks for everything. I really appreciate you looking out for us." Eureka leaned inside of the window and kissed him sweetly on the cheek. The old man blushed.

"Alright now, you guys take it easy." Mr. Rifkins threw the Toyota pickup into reverse. "Reka, you call me if you need anything, okay? I'm just one phone call away."

She nodded and clapped the roof of his truck. They waved goodbye until he was out of sight.

They climbed the staircase and made way for their motel room. As they drew near, they could hear music within a nearby room. At first he couldn't distinguish what the song was, but then it sunk in and he began to mumble the lyrics to himself.

Chief Keef's *'Love Sosa'* seeped from the cracked door of the motel room. Approaching, Anton made out an ashy hand with long finger nails holding the door. He overheard the man saying something to his homeboy as he held the door open.

"Fuck you going, Ralo?" The homeboy asked.

"Shiieet, I'm finna take it to the ATM," Ralo replied. "A nigga tryna get streezy toneezy, ya feel me?"

"Yo, bring back a pack of Cigarillos," homeboy told him.

"Gimmie the money."

"Hold on."

As they crossed the path of the cracked open door, they saw thick, shapely women dancing provocatively with one another. One was bronze and the other was cinnamon brown. They kissed one another thirstily as they held onto clear plastic cups of brown liquor. It was obvious to them that there was a party going on inside of the room of some sort. The man got the money from his homeboy and closed the door shut. He stole a glance at Anton and threw his head back.

"What's up, lil' homie?"

"What up?" Anton spoke.

The man then looked to Eureka, winked and puckered his lips. She rolled her eyes and kept it moving.

Eureka crossed the window of the motel room besides hers and noticed that the blinds were slightly cracked open. Peering through the openings of the blinds she saw two cats sitting at a table. One of them was counting money while the other was cocking crack on a single burner. The cat counting the money looked up and saw her looking in through the openings of the blinds. He shot her a dirty look and twisted the blinds closed.

Eureka opened the door to the motel room and flipped on the light switch. She and Anton stood in the doorway looking over the room. Surprisingly, it was neat and clean. She closed the door shut and they dropped their backpacks on the floor. At the same time they took off for the beds, diving onto them. Smiles spread across their faces as they lay on their backs, staring up at the ceiling with their hands clasped behind their heads.

"Man, this bed is a hell of a lot better than that sofa bed at home," she said.

"You ain't never lied. Let's see what's on TV," Anton picked up the remote control and turned on the television set. Flipping through the channels, he came across something that intrigued her.

"Hold up, Ant, go back," she told him. "Channel 5."

"I'm not tryna watch no news," Anton frowned.

"Do like I said, Punk!" Eureka threw a pillow at his head.

He smacked his lips and changed the channel.

She was found inside of her Hollywood home where she was brutally murdered. Apparently, her head and face had been beaten with a water pipe until it caved in. The pipe was left on the scene and the police plan to run ballistics on it in hopes that it leads them to their suspect...

"This is a cold world." Anton shook her head sadden by what had happened to the girl. "You've gotta really hate a bitch to beat her shit in like that."

"That's some serial killa type shit."

"What do you think was up with this situation, sis?"

Eureka sat up in bed and picked up the steel she'd taken from Malvo. She ejected the magazine from the bottom of the weapon and checked to see how many bullets she had left. Once she was done, she smacked the magazine back into the bottom of the Glock and slid it under her pillow.

"That broad either owed the wrong nigga money, or set a nigga up to get took for some paper." Eureka gave her analysis as she kicked off her Timberland boots and lay back on the bed, resting her head on the pillow.

Anton stacked two of those flat ass motel pillows on top of one another and laid his head back on them as well. He then folded his hands at his stomach.

"Ain't no regular nigga done no shit like that, sis? Uh uh," he shook his head. "That right there is pure evil. That right there is the Devil's work."

Anton went back to flip through the channels looking for something else to watch while she lay back in bed. She was as silent as a grave as she allowed his words marinate inside of her mind. He was right. Only a truly wicked person had to have done that girl like that.

I hope that I don't ever run into a bitch like that, she thought.

Chapter 10

Bemmy sat inside of The Olive Garden eating a Caesar salad. Off to the side sat a glass of ice water with a slice of lemon. He didn't drink any sodas or juices, and he stayed away from pork. As a matter of fact, the only meat he ate was baked fish and chicken. Bemmy was a self-proclaimed health guru that took good care of his body which explained his lean and muscular build. He was razorblade sharp in a charcoal gray pinstriped tailor-made suit and a pair of Fennix alligator shoes that looked like they had been spit shined. Hugging his wrist was a Franck Muller watch. It was simple yet classy.

Bemmy's bodyguard leaned over and whispered something into his ear as he eyeballed the entrance. He looked up from his salad and saw Fear coming through the door. He took a sip of his ice water, then sat it down. Bemmy then picked up the napkin and wiped his mouth. When Fear approached, he rose to his feet and gave him a firm handshake before sitting back down. He went back to eating his salad as he talked with him.

"What's up, Kirby?" Fear addressed Bemmy's bodyguard, throwing his head back.

"Ain't shit, just cooling," Kirby answered.

"How're things going, O.G?" Fear asked.

"Not too good," Bemmy replied. "If they were, you wouldn't be sitting here."

"Makes plenty sense. What chu got for me?"

"A lil' gangbanging dipshit that dared to put his ball scratchers on my baby girl," Bemmy answered. "He did a real number on her, too. This mothafucka makes Ike Turner look like a goddamn choirboy." He looked to Kirby and said, "Show 'em what that cock sucka did to my Bell."

Kirby pulled a cell phone from inside his suit's jacket and handed it to Fear, showing him how to go through the pictures.

He scrolled through the pictures that were taken at different angles. Each picture appeared to be worse than the last. Both of Bell's eyes were swollen shut, the side of her head was twice its size and her nose was broken. Her lips were busted and her two front teeth were chipped. "Damn, I'm sorry this happened," Fear sympathized, handing the cell phone back to Kirby.

"Not as sorry as that son of bitch is going to be," Bemmy swore.

"If this cat put his hands on your daughter, he must not have known that you were her father."

"Oh, he knew," Bemmy assured him. "She told him all about me and the kind of man that I am. He said that he didn't care 'bout what I put down back in the day, it's about now. So, I want you to show him that '73's Bemmy ain't much different from 2014's Bemmy."

"However you want me to serve this nigga, he's gonna get his last meal."

"I brought you a lil' something," Bemmy nodded to two Styrofoam containers. He set the fork down on his plate and laid back in his seat, taking casual sips of his water.

Fear's forehead wrinkled when he saw the containers wondering what was inside of them. He looked back up at Bemmy and he gave him a slight nod. He opened up the first one and saw an 8x10 photograph of the dude who'd made the mistake of winding up on Bemmy's shit list. He was a stocky dude with a face and body like Brian Pumper. He had menacing dark brown eyes, a goatee and an old scar on his cheek. Fear turned the photograph over and saw an address written in red marker.

"Is this an address where I can possibly find 'em?" he looked up from the address.

Bemmy sat his glass of water down after taking a sip and said, "Yeah. He's gotta lil' trap over there in Watts. It's on 105th and Juniper, a two story house. Real cruddy looking place."

"Okay, this shouldn't be to hard to find." He turned the photograph over to take another look at the woman beater's face.

"I want you to do him up real nice. Don't show his woman-beatin'-ass no mercy," Bemmy told him. "Once you've made him suffer, shut his lights out and make sure he knows it was I that sent you to do the deed."

"Alright," Fear nodded and opened the other container. Inside, there were stacks of money secured by rubber-bands.

"It's 25K a head, right? Half up front?" Bemmy asked.

"Yeah, I'll be contacting you, shortly."

"Alright now, take it easy," Bemmy told him.

Fear picked up the containers and headed for the exit.

******

Constance sat back in the driver seat sucking on the end of a square as she waited for Fear to return. This was how they played it when they were contacted for business. She would play the shadows while he met with the client. They did it this way so that the client would be left unaware of Fear having a partner. That way if his client tried to renege on a contract or set him up they wouldn't expect her to swing into action, laying bodies down. It was always best to play it safe. *Never let your right hand know what your left hand is doing* was how Fear explained it.

Constance thought back to a few nights ago when she'd laid her murder game down. She'd killed many people in her line of work, so taking a life was as easy as taking a shit. She thought about the last bitch she laid to rest…..

Brandi came through the door of her house hanging up her purse and kicking off her flats. She pulled off her coat and

106

threw it over the back of the couch. She picked up the remote control and turned on the 42" LG flat-screen. She flicked through the channels until she found something that she wouldn't mind watching. Once she came across The Usual Suspects, she escalated the volume and tossed the remote control onto the coffee table. Brandi sang Drake's 'From Time' as she walked down the hall, unzipping the back of her skirt as she went along. She was about to walk into the bathroom when she noticed that the window was cracked open at the end of the corridor. She frowned and approached the window, closing it shut and locking it. Thinking that she'd heard something, she froze where she was and her brow furrowed as she listened for it again.

"Humph," Brandi shrugged her shoulders before entering the bathroom and flipping on the light switch. When the light didn't come on, she flipped it off and on rapidly, but it still didn't come on. Nothing. Frustrated, she exhaled and stomped her foot. "Damn it, this light done blew out again? Shit!" she exasperated. This would have been the third time she'd changed the light bulb in the bathroom this week. She didn't know what the problem was but she planned on calling an electrician to come out tomorrow since she didn't have to go to work the next day. As soon as Brandi got the notion to turn around, something sharp jabbed her in her eye. "Agh," she held her eye as she staggered back into the hall and bumped into the wall. Brandi opened her injured eye and couldn't see anything out of it, she had been blinded. She touched her wounded eye and her trembling hand came away sticky with blood. Hearing a feral snarl, her head snapped up and she unleashed a scream so loud that her uvula shook at the back of her throat.

A hooded figure leapt forth from the darkness of the bathroom, cloaked in black army fatigues. Constance attacked Brandi with a viciousness that hadn't been seen since the medieval times era. She grunted as she swung a small bladed weapon back and forth across Brandi's face. Brandi's face opened up to the white bloody meat like it was being unzipped. When she lifted her hands up, Constance continued to assault her, swinging the blade as hard and as fast as she could. Brandi's palms split open and she narrowed her eyes to shield them from the specs of blood jumping out at her face. Brandi staggered down the hall holding her eye and dragging her other hand along the wall, leaving smears of blood. Constance stalked her prey with a calm head, there was no rush, Brandi would get what was coming to her.

Brandi rounded the corner and staggered into the living room. Constance was right on her trail. She dropped the blade and unzipped her army jacket, withdrawing a length of pipe. She tapped the length of pipe in her gloved palm as she advanced on Brandi. Brandi had just picked up the telephone when the heavy pipe slammed into the side of her knee. She howled out in blinding excruciation and her mouth dropped open. The sensation was so overwhelming that it had literally sucked the next breath out of her lungs. Brandi whipped around and she swung the pipe down on her shoulder, snapping her collar bone like a chicken bone. She fell to the floor crawling toward the door with tears streaming from the corners of her eyes.

"I bet chu won't fuck with another bitch's man after today, hoe. I guarantee that." Constance stood over her as she made her futile attempt to escape her wrath. She struck Brandi in the back with the pipe causing her eyes to bulge and her to croak in pain. The crippling blow immobilized Brandi and stopped her dead in her tracks.

"Oh, my God!" She grimaced in agony, tears falling rapidly down her cheeks. She couldn't move and was sure that her spinal cord had been damaged. Constance pulled Brandi over so she could see her face.

"No, not God—the Devil," Constance pulled the black bandana from the lower half of her face, revealing her identity

and exposing a devilish smile. When Brandi saw who her attacker was she pissed on herself. She never expected for things to be taken this far over some dick, but what she didn't know was that some chicks were willing to take it there and even further for what they felt belonged to them.

Her mother had always told her that she was going to pay one day for always trying to fuck with somebody's man. She knew that it was most likely true, but she never expected to be paying with her life.

Brandi looked off to the side at the ceiling to floor mirror. She had what she could only akin to an outer body experience. It was as if she wasn't there but at a theater eating popcorn and watching her own movie. She was hurting so bad that she couldn't wait for this last scene to fade out and the credits to roll.

Brandi saw Constance standing over her with the pipe gripped firmly in her hand. She could also see the boots that she wore. They were Timberlands.

"I heard you like them long, fat and black," Constance spoke of the pipe she held as if it were a dick. "Well, here ya go!"

Whoomp!

Constance swung the pipe down into Brandi's face, breaking her eye socket and dotting her eye red. When she swung it a second time, a sickening crunch was heard and her skull split. From there it was murder she wrote as she swung the pipe into Brandi's skull. She heard the bone crack and saw the skin come apart like the loose threads of a seam. Specs of blood clung to Constance's face and clothes, but she continued with the merciless brutality you would think only came from a barbarian. The more blood flew, the tighter Constance squeezed her eyes shut and the harder she swung. Once blood splattered against the flat-screen TV and Brandi's face looked like bloody ground beef, she tossed the crimson stained pipe aside. For a time, she stood over her on her knees taking labored breaths as she studied her handiwork, tilting her head to the side for better observation.

Constance got to her feet and shuffled to the door. She pulled the door open and left as quietly as she came. The last scene of The Usual Suspects played on the flat-screen.

The greatest trick that the Devil pulled was convincing the world that he didn't exist, and like that—he was gone.

Brandi wasn't the first to meet with The Grim Reaper behind Fear. There was Desiree, Trishelle, Gloria, Chyna, Taraji, and Unique. Desiree got strangled to death. Trishelle took three to the dome at a stop-light. Gloria got her throat slit. Chyna was poisoned. Taraji got hers through a car bomb and Unique was shoved off of the roof of a building.

Constance put the smash on all of those hoes without any remorse. She didn't take pity on a soul. If a bitch so much as batted her eyes at Fear, she took it as them smiling at him with their pussies. She obliterated her competition by making their deaths quick but bloody, then getting the fuck out of the way.

Constance did what she did out of love. If she couldn't have him, then no one could. He was all she had in the world and she didn't want anyone swooping in and snatching him from out of her life. If she lost him, she wasn't sure that she could get over it. Just the thought of it made her sick. She had it bad for him and didn't think that she'd ever be able to shake him loose.

Constance unlocked the door from the panel when she saw him approach. He snatched the front passenger door open and deposited himself in the seat. She fired up the BMW 640i and pulled out of the parking lot. Occasionally, she'd glanced over at Fear and the photograph he was examining.

"Who we got?" she asked of the cat on the picture.

"Reginald Burson. His Alias is Bugsy. I wanna see where this place is tonight, so swing by there."

"What's the address?" she questioned.

Fear read off the address and she punched it into the navigational system. Thirty-five minutes later, she was pulling up on the block and killing the engine. They arrived on Juniper. The light posts on the street illuminated so dimly it looked as if the block was submerged in darkness. Every now and again a car would drive past or the shadows would stir with someone shuffling about.

Constance slumped down in the seat along with Fear, trying to be incognito.

"Are you sure that this it?" she asked.

"Yeah, this is the spot," he answered.

A dope fiend had shuffled up to the door of the trap and knocked in a very specific pattern. A couple of minutes later, the door opened and a bulky stud in a beanie and gold Rolex chain peered out, scanning the area.

Fear looked up from the photograph to the bulky stud that had just stepped foot out on the porch.

"That's him."

"Let me see that," Constance took the picture, looking at it and then the bulky stud. She agreed, it was him.

"You wanna take 'em?"

"Nah, Bemmy doesn't want us to just murk this nigga. He wants us to torture 'em 'fore we make 'em part with his life."

"Right."

"Besides, I'm sure he's gotta couple of niggaz in there to watch his back. We'd do better falling back until we're able to gather some Intel. Figure out the layout of the place and how many niggaz he has on deck. What kind of iron they're toting, the specifics." He removed the wrapper from a stick of Winter Fresh gum and stuck it into his mouth. Glancing in the side-view mirror, he spotted a shabbily dressed man ambling up the sidewalk pushing a shopping cart full of bagged cans, bottles, and an assortment of other junk. Fear rubbed his chin as he thought about something. He dipped his hand into his pocket and pulled out a few neatly folded bills. He pulled a Benjamin free and returned the folded bills to his pocket.

"What're you about to do?"

"You'll see."

Fear hopped out of the car and hustled over to the man. Through the rearview mirror, Constance watched Fear give him the hundred dollar bill before they ducked off into a neighboring alley. A couple of minutes later when they emerged they were wearing one another's clothes.

A smirk formed on Constance's lips as it dawned on her what he had in mind. She watched as he stuck a Blu-Tooth behind his ear and threw the hood of his hoodie over his head. He gave her a slight nod as he shuffled passed the car and headed into the yard of the trap. Hearing her cell phone ring, she looked at its screen and saw that it was Fear. She stuck her Blu-Tooth behind her ear, answered the call and listened in as he approached the door of the trap. She watched him knock on the door just how they'd seen the dope fiend do not long ago. Not long after he was granted entrance into the domain by Bugsy himself. Excited, she sat up in the driver's seat rubbing her hands together and listening in.

"You okay?" she asked in a low tone so no one would hear her on his end.

"Yeah, he's taking me to cop now," Fear replied in the same tone as she. "Man, this place is like a living, breathing nightmare. Modern day Sodom & Gomorrah. Alright, I just copped me a space to squat. I'ma kick it in here for a minute to act like I'm getting high."

"Okay. I'ma stay on in case there's drama."

"Roger that."

Constance took her .45 automatic from the stash box and screwed the silencer on it. She tucked it between the seat and the console. She then laid back in the driver seat listening closely. If shit went left, she was running up in that thang giving niggaz tough talk and hot slugs. Twenty minutes later,

Fear emerged from the trap keeping a close eye on his surroundings. He walked past the car in case someone was watching. He ducked beside a blue van. On his bending knees he hurried over to the passenger side of the BMW. He pulled the door open and stashed himself in the front passenger seat.

"Jesus," her nose scrunched up and she whipped her head away from Fear, holding a hand over her nose and mouth.

"It's these clothes, huh?" Fear smirked, pinching his hoodie and taking a whiff. He looked like he ate something sour after smelling the funk in it. "Yeah, these mothafuckaz are ripe. Pull over in that alley behind us so that I can toss these duds."

Gripping her .45 automatic tightly, Constance played lookout as Fear stepped out of the car and pulled off the hoodie and trench coat. He tossed the duds aside amongst a pile of black garbage bags and hopped back inside of the car.

"How many were in there?"

"Including Bugsy? Five." Fear answered, trying to pull a splinter out of his middle-finger. "Two upstairs and three below. The ones downstairs tote Tecs and the two upstairs are holding Uzis."

"What're you thinking?"

"Piece of cake, we got this."

"Nigga, you say that about every job."

Fear grinned but his brow quickly furrowed as he continued to try to pull the splinter free from his middle-finger.

Seeing him struggle, Constance leaned closer and took his hand. "Let me see." Without much effort, she plucked the splinter out of his finger and flicked it away.

"Aren't chu gonna kiss it and make it all better?" he asked.

"I'll do you one better," she replied. Keeping eye contact with him, she sucked his middle-finger slowly and seductively as if it were a dick. The warmth and wetness of her mouth sliding up and down his finger caused his fuck organ to shift and sprout until it was standing up like a flower that had been watered and given plenty of sunlight. He grunted, dying to feel what her insides felt like. The thought alone made his fuck organ grow slightly harder and press up against the inside of his zipper.

Constance sucking his middle-finger awoke the beast inside of Fear. It was a beast that once unleashed something had to die, that something was going to be her pussy. *R.I.P.*

Fear grabbed the inside of the collar of her t-shirt and with a strong tug, ripped it down the middle. Constance's supple breasts spilled free. They were slightly saggy but just as beautiful as he'd remembered them. He took a breast in each palm, admiring their perfect sculpts as he tested their weight. They were absolutely gorgeous. Their chocolate areolas were inviting, they called his name. *Fear...Fearr...Fearrrr.* He imagined hearing their soft whispers.

No longer able to tame himself, he attacked those bad boys savagely. Fear licked, sucked, and gently pulled on the nipples with his teeth. His tampering of her breasts drew soft moans from Constance. She threw her head back and closed her eyes. Licking her top lip, she rubbed the back of his head and she looked down at him. As he gave her breasts their worth in attention, she could literally feel her juices soaking her thong.

"Sssss, I need it, baby. I need it. I need it now!" she moaned sensually.

"Tell me what chu need, baby?" Fear said between sucking and lapping at her clit. He was so smooth and skilled that she hadn't even felt him slip off her cargo pants and thong. Constance had to admit that he was blowing her mind right then. She needed that dick like a gunshot victim needed an ambulance.

114

"That—that—dick!" she whined, biting her inner jaw as she had an orgasm. Constance sat scrunched in the driver seat, legs wide open, and shivering from some mean ass head. Fear sat up, unzipped his jeans and released his steel. That mothafucka stood long, fat, black and ready to kill something. He removed the golden foil wrapper of a Magnum and pulled out the slick Jimmie hat. He rolled that bitch down on his dick and looked to her.

"Hop your ass into the backseat, and hurry the fuck up!" he ordered like the boss nigga he was.

"Yes, Daddy." Constance climbed into the backseat and he smacked her ass causing her left cheek to jiggle. As she climbed over the console, he noticed her pussy raining hot juices on the cup-holder.

"Lay yo mothafucking ass back and keep them legs wide open. I'm finna get all up in them guts," he said with a hard face letting her know that he wasn't fucking around as he stroked his pole.

Once Constance had done what he'd ordered her to do, he climbed into the backseat and pulled her closer. After spreading her long sexy legs further apart, he eased himself inside of her inch by inch, filling up that warm, wet, tight, sweet hole of hers. It took all of his self-control to stop from busting off too quick. Her shit was just that fucking fire.

Fuck she put in this pussy? This mothafucka is off the chain.

Fear pushed the thought of how good Constance's pussy felt from out of his mind. He put a fist on each side of her and positioned himself for balance. She reached above her head and gripped the handle dangling from the ceiling near the backdoor. She braced herself in anticipation for a thorough dick down.

Fear threw his hooked shaped dick into her wet darkness, laying into her long and strong. Each and every last one of his powerful, lust filled thrust caused the Charger to

115

rock back and forth. Once he established a rhythm, it was on like Donkey Kong.

Constance turned her head to the side as her eyes rolled to their whites. Her lips peeled apart and she looked up at him, seeing that he was enjoying their fucking just as much as she was.

"Ahhh! Ahhh! Shit! Get this mothafucking pussy! Beat this shit up! Ohhhhhh, my Lord Jesusssss!" Her legs shook as she welcomed another orgasm. It was so good that she died, came back, and was looking to experience it all over again.

The sex was intense, powerful, passionate and so hot that the steam exhausting from their bodies fogged the windows and masked the glass like early morning dew. Warm droplets of sweat splashed against Constance's breasts and neck. Lifting her head up from the black leather seats, she licked and nibbled on Fear's nipples. This intensified the sex for him. He threw his head back and his eyelids fluttered.

He pumped inside of her faster, and faster, chasing after that nut he so desperately wanted as if it were his next breath. Her juices rolled down the length of his meaty pole and dripped like a leaky faucet onto the black leather seats. He arched his back, dipping in and out of her slicken tightness. He grunted, feeling the walls of her second mouth grip him, pulling him in like quick sand. Each time he dove in and out he could feel his male mayonnaise drawing near. Finally, after three last strokes he erupted, spilling his seeds inside of the condom.

Exhausted, he collapsed on top of her. Their wet bodies nestled against one another. She laid one hand to his lower back while the other caressed his head, lovingly. She closed her eyes wishing that he was her man, but he wasn't. And the truth of the matter was that he may never be. She didn't mind for the moment though, she just wanted to enjoy him   for   the   time   being.

Tranay Adams

Chapter 11

Once Malvo saw to it that Faith and Heaven were safe and sound at her parents' house out in Rancho Cucamonga, he and his goons hopped back onto the 210 heading West back to the City of Watts. Taking the 10 exit and getting off on Wilmington Avenue, they acknowledged that the sun was emerging and the sky was turning gray. When they rolled up into The Jordan Downs projects they saw his Chevy parked. It was little more than a hunk of charcoal as it had been burned. The ground surrounding it was scorched black. Malvo sat up in his seat when he saw his ride. His eyebrows arched and his lips peeled open in shock.

"My baby," he uttered. It pained him to see his Pretty Black Bitch ruined.

"Damn, that's yo shit?" Crunch asked.

"That mothafucka ain't nothing but a hunk of coal now." Ronny said.

"Stop, stop the truck!" Malvo commanded. When Crunch stopped the truck, he hopped out and ran over to his burnt Chevy. You would have thought he was at the morgue viewing the body of his mother how devastated he was. The expression on his face was one of a man that had his heart pierced by a dagger.

Malvo circled around the Chevy touching it as if he would hurt it if he pressed against it too hard. His eyes became glassy and he wanted to cry seeing his Pretty Black Bitch like that, but the gangster in him kept his emotions in a chokehold. He looked up from car just as Crunch and Ronny had hopped out of the truck and approached. Some of the tenants had emerged from out of their homes.

"Who done this to her? I wanna know right now, goddamn it!" Malvo spat furiously, jabbing the air with his finger. His eyes darted around at all of the faces. Some were

118

solemn, some hostile, others straight. "Oh, y'all don't know nothing, huh? Didn't nobody hear nothing while they were out here flame broiling my shit? Alright, if that's how we doing it, then cool! But trust and believe that somebody's gone answer for this," he swore, drawing his steel and waving Crunch and Ronny along as he advanced in the direction of The Jackson's apartment.

Seeing the trio approaching, a little nigga struck through the crowd hauling ass across the courtyard. To anyone observing him it looked like he was running away, but he was actually going to get someone.

Unbeknownst to Malvo and his goons, two niggaz on the roof of The Jackson's tenement peered over the ledge down at them.

Boom!

The door of The Jackson's apartment flew open sending a spray of splinters across the living room. The trio fanned out, each one taking a room. They checked high and low, searching every crack and crevasse leaving no stone unturned. When they concluded that no one was home, Malvo and Ronny joined back up inside of the living room.

"They must have gotten ghost that same night," Ronny told Malvo.

"That's a smart lil' bitch. She knows my get down," Malvo said, staring off at nothing as he slipped a square between his lips. He tucked his steel onto his waistline and patted his person down for a lighter.

"I got chu," Ronny tucked his burner and pulled out a Bic. He cupped his hand around the cigarette and sparked that bitch up, smoke wafted.

"This is her?" Crunch emerged from Eureka and Anton's bedroom with a portrait of a younger her.

Malvo turned around expelling smoke and taking the portrait from him. He nodded his head and said, "Yeah, this is her," he then broke the glass on the pointed corner of the

The Devil Wears Timbs

living room's television set and pulled the photograph free from the shattered glass. He let the frame of the photograph drop to the floor and flapped the loose glass from off it. Once he was done he folded the picture and tucked it into the inside pocket of his leather jacket.

"Let's get the fuck outta here." Malvo exited the apartment with his goons. The sun was shining now and their eyes squinted under the rays of the reddish orange marble residing over the projects.

"Malvo." A voice came from somewhere within the crowd of tenants that had been watching them ever since they entered their domain. Malvo took the square from his lips, expelling smoke from his nostrils and mouth as his eyes eagerly searched the crowd.

"I'm right here, cuz." The crowd began to stir as someone moved amongst them. Suddenly, an older gangster emerged flanked by six Baby Locs. He sported a baldhead and a goatee littered with gray hairs. He rocked black sunglasses to cover the eye he'd lost in a shootout when he was in the streets young and thugging. A purple tank top clung to his slim, well defined muscular body.

"Loc Dog?" Malvo peered closely.

"That's Mr. Loc Dog to you, homeboy." Loc Dog spoke from where he stood. His muscles made him look like a black superhero. But that assumption would be wrong. The Dog didn't fight crime, he participated in it. "I heard you've been terrorizing my people since I've been gone. Well, a nigga home now, fresh off a bid. And I'm here to tell you that that shit gone stop!" It seemed as if guns were appearing out of thin air as all of the Baby Locs with Loc Dog were suddenly pulling them. Malvo and his goons looked around on high alert. They knew that they were outnumbered and outgunned. He decided to choose his words wisely because if not, he and his goons would be pushing up daisies in the time it would take to pull a trigger.

120

"Alright, you got this one." Malvo bowed out gracefully.

"I know I do," Loc Dog's face oozed with the contempt he felt for him. "What the fuck else are you gone do but bleed to death if you front? You in my world, Jones, I'll make you my bitch!"

"Man, fuck this nigga!" Crunch growled. He went to lift his banger, but Malvo grabbed his wrist. Looking into his eyes, Malvo shook his head.

"Don't be stupid. We can't win this one," he stated sternly.

"He's right, Crunch, these dudes got us dead to rights," Ronny reasoned.

Crunch assessed the situation and nodded, keeping his banger at his side.

"Bounce niggaz, 'fore I break the sixth commandment, *Thou Shall Not Kill*," he commanded, trailing behind him and his goons as they headed toward the parking lot.

Malvo mad dogged Loc Dog from behind the glass of the backseat window. Suddenly, Malvo pressed his middle-finger against the glass showing a lack of respect for the O.G. "Okay, alright, cuz, The Dog tried to be peaceful," he looked to the roof of The Jackson's tenement, put his fingers at the corners of his mouth and whistled. Malvo's forehead creased with worried lines and he tried to see what Loc Dog was looking at as Crunch backed out of the parking space. Malvo couldn't see what was going on but he would soon feel it.

The niggaz on the roof emerged wearing purple bandanas over the lower halves of their faces. They aimed their M-16 assault rifles at the top of the truck and brought in the 4th of July early. Bullets pelted the roof of the truck making Malvo and his goons slide down in their seats. Crunch was almost on the floor as he maneuvered the truck out of the projects. Hot-ones whizzed through the windshield peppering the dashboard with broken glass. The grill of the truck came apart as it was struck by an onslaught of bullets and its front driver side tire burst.

"Welcome to Watts, mothafuckaz. Don't bring ya asses back across them train tracks!" Loc Dog threw up his set. He watched the truck speed away. Its passengers barely escaping with their lives. "Mark ass niggaz!" he spat on the ground and headed back inside of The Jordan's, giving his Baby Locs three high fives. The projects residents gave him praise and rounds of applause.

"Are y'all alright?" Malvo sat up in the backseat, looking between Crunch and Ronny.

"I'm good," Ronny answered. He looked to Crunch, "You good, Crunch?"

Crunch nodded, "I'm straight. Just feeling like a straight up punk for letting them fools blast on us like that."

"Don't wet that shit, Loc Dog gone get his but right now I've got bigger fish to fry," Malvo told him. "We need to get this big bastard off of the streets 'cause if The Ones see this mothafucka shot full of holes like this they for sure gone pull us over, and we can't afford to have that happen riding dirty."

"My Auntie doesn't live too far from here. I know she'll let us stash it inside of her garage."

"Cool. That's where we're at with it."

After stashing the Escalade in Crunch's aunt's garage, they borrowed her '98 Pontiac Grand Prix and headed out on to Firestone Street. Firestone Street was known for its independent car lots. There were car lots lined up and down the block on both sides. Sometimes you could catch some privately owned cars out on the streets for sale for a cool ass price.

Malvo copped a milk white '04 Chevy Tahoe truck. He broke the owner off and climbed in behind the wheel while Crunch hopped into the front passenger seat. He had a plug at the DMV in Inglewood so he was headed out there now to handle the paper work. He knew that he was most likely going to end up doing some dirt in it so he was going to have it registered to a fake name and address. He'd been doing this shit since before he could piss straight. So for him it was just like another day at the office.

"Yo, Ronny, as soon as you get back hit my jack, fam." Malvo said, making his hand into the shape of a telephone.

"I got chu," Ronny stuck his hand out of the window and touched fists with Malvo before pulling off. Malvo had just dropped a few bands into Ronny's lap for a couple of birds of heroin. He had planned on stretching that work and dumping it on his blocks to get them back jumping. After he paid off his workers, he was going to flip that paper more than a high school cheerleader at practice. That was the only way he saw himself being able to pay the Greeks off.

Pulling up at a red stop-light, Malvo pulled the photograph of Eureka from inside of his leather jacket. Unfolding it, he looked it over. *I don't know where you are but I'm going to find you. And I'm going to take what you owe me in blood.*

Chapter 12
One Week Later

Eureka sat on the steps in deep thought as she casually smoked a cigarette. These past few days had been hectic and the nicotine was just what she needed to calm her nerves. She didn't know what her next move was going to be. She was running low on money. She had enough dough for another week's stay at the motel and a week's worth of food if she budgeted right. After that, she didn't have a clue on what she was going to do. She didn't just have herself to look after, but her baby brother as well. It was up to her to provide a stable place to live and put food on the table. These were the responsibilities of a single mother and she was going to have to fulfill them.

Eureka figured that she had two choices. She could cop seven grams of coke and flip it, or she could run up in somebody's shit and make them lay it down. Giving how hot the hood was she knew that slinging was out of the question for her. If she was to get popped, she'd be sent to jail and Anton would be sent to foster care. Not to mention she'd more than likely spend hours posted up trying to get it. Eureka needed hers not now but right now, so she was going to don that ski-mask and that banger like Batman did his cape and cowl. She already had a gun so now she had to get herself something that could conceal her identity. Though she was leaning towards a ski-mask, a bandana was more acquirable given the neck of the woods she was in. Eureka knew that she could walk into any liquor store and buy a bandana, but to get her hands on a ski-mask she most likely would have to go to a department store.

Now that she had her hustle figured out, she had to find her prey. She was starving, so a mid-level hustler would do at this time until she'd gotten herself together to move onto bigger fish. She was going at this alone and she had never robbed anyone before so she was going to need plenty of practice if she was going to get her strategy and technique down pact.

Eureka blew out a cloud of smoke and glanced at her watch. It was 9:30PM and the liquor stores would be closing shortly, so she figured she'd better get on the move now. After mashing out her square and tucking it behind her ear, she told Anton that she was heading to the liquor store. It was cold out, so she pulled a beanie low over her brow and zipped her jacket all of the way up. Bopping toward the stairs, she saw a milk white 2014 Range Rover pull into the motel's parking lot. A slim, high yellow dude who rocked his reddish orange hair in a close fade hopped out toting a JC Penny's shopping mall bag. A small flip cell phone was glued to his ear as he hustled up the stairs. He glanced in Eureka's direction, but kept it pushing. She was making her way down the steps when she heard him talking to someone.

"What it do, Fee?" he spoke. "Nah, this Reggie, fam. Yeah, the twins" he spoke in code, referring to the two kilos of cocaine, "dropped by looking for you. Nah, they aren't gone yet. I'ma try to get 'em to stay a while longer, but chu need to hurry up. One of the homie's may slide through and get 'em. Alright, I'll see ya then. Peace."

Reggie disconnected the call and slipped the flip cell phone back into the pocket of his white Levi's. Eureka watched as he knocked on the door and waited to be let in. A chubby, dark skinned cat with his hair in a Mohawk opened the door for Reggie. Eating a bag of Sunflower Seeds, he took a quick scan of the area.

"Yo, Coal, why don't chu close the door, fam? It's colder than my baby momma's heart out there," she heard Reggie yell.

"Pull your dress down, nigga. You're supposed to be a man," Coal told him. "You in here whining about how cold it is and what not, sounding like a lil' bitch." Coal walked back inside of the motel room, slamming the door shut behind him.

*****

Within two shakes of a lamb's tail, Eureka was back at her room at The Snooty Fox. When she came through the door she found the TV on mute and Anton with his ear pressed up against the wall. From the look on his face she could tell that whatever was being said on the other side of the wall had his undivided attention. With swift movements of his hand, Anton directed Eureka to listen at the wall.

"What's up?"

"I heard some bumping around over there. I'm tryna see what's going on," he whispered.

She sat her plastic black bag of items on the table by the window and pressed her ear against the wall.

"Coal, you need to get that Play station off of the floor. I damn near broke my neck," Reggie complained.

"My fault, fam. You alright?"

"I'll live," he answered. "Ya boy, Fee, gone be here in a minute to get these two joints," they heard Reggie tell Coal. "Old boy I met at the gallery, Bo-D, he talking about picking up one."

"Shit, I already broke that *one* down," Coal informed Reggie. "Them fools around the corner want a couple of zones."

"Man, fuck them fools around the corner," Reggie told Coal. "We get rid of these three and we're done. We could have been done burned through these three joints."

"Yeah, I guess you're right," Coal said. "I hollered at my girl's cousin. He said he can hit us with some joints for the low."

"How much?"

"Nineteen."

126

"Alright, I can fuck with that," Reggie said. "Down the road we're gone have to negotiate, though."

"Man," Coal said, sounding like he was worried.

"What's up, Foolie?"

"My uncle," Coal told him. "I know that nigga gone come at us with everything he's got."

"I doubt it. That's your aunt's husband, right?" Reggie asked. "If he catches up with us he'll probably just throw you a beat down since you're family. But me on the other hand, he'll probably body me to teach me a lesson. But I'm not wetting it though, 'cause if any niggaz come my way I'm sending 'em back in body bags. Before they kill me they gone feel me, straight up."

"I hear you, my nigga, and my gun gone be right besides yours," Coal pledged his allegiance.

"That's love, my nigga," Reggie responded.

They pulled their ears away from the wall.

"You hear that, sis? That's money in the bank." Anton rubbed his hands together greedily. "All we gotta do is run up in there and make them Fuck-Boys lay it down."

"I'ma get down, but you aren't coming along for the ride," she told him.

"What?" Anton frowned. "It was my idea."

"The hell it was." Eureka said, pulling a black bandana from her bag of items. "I been had the idea to bring it to them dudes. That's why I brought this for my disguise."

"Aww, come on, Reka, let me be down."

"Nuh uh, Ant, I don't wanna risk you getting hurt, or even worse—killed." Eureka said, staring at her reflection in the mirror as she pulled a black sweatshirt over her head.

"The same thing could happen to you."

"Yeah, well, I'm taking this risk for the both of us."

"You're gonna need someone to watch your back. There's two of 'em in there. You think they aren't packing?

They're gonna be prepared for something like that. So, you're gonna need me. I can be the eyes in the back of your head."

Eureka paused as she slipped the $5 dollar liquor store shades onto her face. Anton could tell that she was at least thinking about it.

"Nah, Ant. I only got one gun, anyway."

"What about this?" Anton pulled out the black cap-gun.

"It's not real." Eureka responded, tying the black bandana over the lower half of her face.

"I know that." He aimed the cap-gun at a lamp sitting on a nightstand on the other side of the room. "It's not real, but it looks real. When they see it they gone think I'm holding steel and will be hesitant to try anything."

She blew hard as she tossed the thought around inside of her head. Against her better judgment she decided to let Anton in on the lick. She had to admit that he was right. She was stepping into a den of lions and would need someone to watch her back. And even though his gun wouldn't be real the cats they were robbing wouldn't know it. As long as he went in with his game face on and let them niggaz know that they meant business then things would be as smooth as silk.

"Alright," she agreed.

"We on." A mischievous smile spread across his face. He licked his lips and rubbed his hands together greedily.

"Here." Eureka tossed him the extra camouflage bandana she'd bought. "Put that on."

She watched as Anton put on a black hoodie and tied the camouflage bandana over the lower half of his face. He stood beside her in the mirror and they looked themselves over. They pointed their weapons at their reflections and practiced their tough faces.

"You ready?"

"Hell yeah, let's do this." He seriously stated.

"Alright then, this is what I want you to do…" Eureka went on to rundown the plan.

*****

Reggie was stretched across the bed watching *The Game* while taking pulls from a thinly rolled L. He blew smoke rings into the air and watched as they dissipated before it reached the ceiling. Coal sat at the table repackaging a kilo of coke with latex gloved hands. Once he'd finally gotten the kilo resealed, a smile surfaced on his face and he wiped the beads of sweat from his forehead with the back of his hand.

"What chu think, Reg?" Coal held up the kilo for Reggie to see. Reggie nodded and gave him a thumb up. Coal placed the kilo back into the JC Penny's shopping bag along with the other three. A knock at the door caused Coal and Reggie's necks to snap in the direction of the door. Reggie pressed the mute button on the TV and sat up. He went to draw iron and Coal stopped him.

"Chill, it's probably just Fee." Coal said, sitting the JC Penny's shopping bag inside of the closet and pulling off the latex gloves as he headed for the door. "Who is it?" he called out as he approached.

"Yo, man, don't one of you guys own a white Range Rover?" the voice said from the other side of the door. "There's a basehead out here tryna break into it."

"Mothafucka," Reggie snatched his weapon from off of the dresser and hopped to his feet. He hurriedly approached the door just as Coal had unlocked and pulled it open.

Boom!

The door slammed into Coal's face breaking his nose and busting his mouth. He stumbled back and hit the floor cupping the lower half of his face. Reggie went to point his weapon but Eureka quickly descended upon him, banger pointed straight at his dome ready to set his skull on fire. Her heart was pounding inside of her chest and she began to sweat like it was ninety-five degrees and sunny inside of the motel room. If she wanted this stickup to go smoothly, she had to get a grip. She had to take control of the situation because if not that was her ass.

"Drop that shit, nigga, or make the L.A Times out this bitch!" Eureka spat with a chill to her tone that let Reggie know she meant business. Reggie complied and she moved in with Anton at her back.

That's it Reka, you've gotta hold of this sitch', sis. Make these niggaz march to the beat of your drum, she thought to herself.

"Don't nobody in here move!" Eureka commanded.

"Y'all heard her," he barked. "A nigga bet not so much as blink!"

"You've gotta be kidding me? What the fuck is this? A joke?" Coal asked with a leaking nose and bloodied teeth.

"Yeah and here's the punch-line." Anton kicked Coal dead in the forehead and sent his head flying back against the wall. When Coal looked up wincing, Anton could see a knot the size of a golf ball forming on his forehead. "You ask anymore dumb ass questions and this .38 special is going to answer them, ya feel me?"

"Close the door." Eureka ordered, keeping her eyes and her banger on Reggie. "Have a seat, homeboy," she instructed him.

Reggie wore a hard face, but did as she said. While Anton tended to Coal, she handled Reggie. "Where the yay at?" she questioned him.

"There ain't no…"

With a movement that was almost a blur, she cracked Reggie in the grill with the butt of her weapon, cutting short the lie he was about to tell. Reggie turned around mad dogging her with red lips. He spat on the floor and a gooey length of red saliva hung from his lip.

"Lie to me again and you'll never have kids," Eureka said with a pair of evil eyes, pointing her banger at Reggie's testicles.

"Reggie, don't tell these mothafuckaz shit!" Coal yelled out. "Fuck them, man!"

"Now I'ma ask you again. Where the yay at?"

Reggie stared her down defiantly, the intensity in his eyes seemed to pierce Eureka's pupils and peer into the core of her soul.

"You heard, my man, bitch! Fuck y'all!" Reggie voice went up an octave as he rushed her. They fell back upon the bed closest to the door and rolled over, hitting the floor. They struggled for control. Anton watched unable to do anything. If he took his eyes off Coal then that would leave them at a total disadvantage. He anxiously awaited the outcome, hoping that his sister would somehow come out on top.

Bloc!

When the first shot went off it startled both Anton and Coal. All was still as if the world had been put on pause. Reggie rose to his feet wearing a sinister smile and clutching the heat. He looked down and saw a black hole in his chest with a red stream running from it. His eyes bulged and his mouth went slack as he touched the wound, bloodying his fingers. He dropped the gun and staggered back, bumping into the bed and sitting down. She came to her feet breathing hard with a heaving chest. Gripping the banger, she pressed it into Reggie's forehead. His eyes snapped open as soon as he felt the bullet's impact.

"Reggie!" Coal bellowed seeing his man's spaghetti splatter against the wall. Chunks of his brain slid down and nestled into the carpet.

"Ol' piss colored nigga." She kicked Reggie's limp leg.

"You alright, sis?"

She nodded.

Seeing that Anton's attention was diverted by Eureka, Coal took advantage of the small window of time. He cracked Anton in the jaw and grabbed his gun. Holding the gun with both hands, he swung it around, and pointed it at her.

"You done fucked up!" He pulled the trigger back to back, and each time it made a *click* sound. A frown enveloped Coal's face and he looked at the gun. That's when he realized that it was a toy gun.

Bloc!

Something hot pierced Coal's neck and he felt blood squirting. He slapped a hand over the spurting wound and clenched his teeth. She kept her weapon trained on Coal, quickly moving in to finish him off.

"When I got in here I specifically said, 'nobody in here move' and I'll be damned if you didn't do exactly what I said not to," she pointed her banger at a wincing Coal's head. "A hardhead makes a soft ass but hot slugs make one dead ass nigga."

Bloc! Bloc!

Two to the helmet and Coal dropped face first into the carpet. Eureka put another one in his thinking cap to make sure that ass wasn't getting up again. She then tucked her piece at the small of her back and helped Anton up to his feet.

"We've gotta get outta here, sis. After all of those shots I know The Ones are on the way."

"We're not going anywhere until we find that yayo."

They searched the motel until they found the JC Penny's shopping bag with the blocks of cocaine in it inside of the closet. *Jackpot!* They smiled behind the bandanas covering the lower halves of their faces.

When Eureka and Anton ran outside there were some guests peeking from between the blinds of their windows and others bold enough to be out on the balcony. Together, they dashed down the balcony and hustled down the steps, hearing the sounds of police sirens flooding the air.

132

Tranay Adams

When they made it off of the motel's grounds, their heads snapped from left to right and saw police cruisers coming from both directions. They ran to their right and sprinted down a residential block where they apprehended an old blue Honda station wagon that Anton had popped the locks on earlier. They eased inside of the Honda station wagon and closed the doors back quietly. Looking through the rearview mirror, they saw the police cruisers racing passed them. They blew a sigh of relief and pulled the bandanas down from over the faces.

Anton hotwired the car and Eureka drove off. They went inside of the motel for a 211 only but left with two 187's.

Chapter 13

After bagging and burning the clothes they'd worn on their caper gone wrong, they took turns washing up inside of a sink in a Chevron gas station bathroom. When it was her turn, she made sure to scrub her fingers nails and hands of any gunpowder residue. Although, she'd worn gloves there may have still been a chance that some traces of gunpowder had clung to her hands.

Once they were done, they dried themselves off with napkins and got dressed. Hungry, they bought a couple of microwavable burritos, chips, and sodas. She parked on 81st and Figueroa, killed the engine and got comfortable as they ate.

"So, where are we going to crash tonight?" Anton asked with a mouthful of burrito.

Eureka chewed and swallowed her food before answering, "Here."

"Here, here? You mean, like in the car?" he asked with raised eyebrows.

"We're wounded right now, money shorter than a midget on its knees."

"Alright," he said disappointedly and took another bite of his burrito.

"Don't trip," Eureka told him. "We'll be alright in a minute. Tomorrow I'ma holla at Spoons and see what's up. I'm sure he'll wanna cop these bricks off us."

"And if that doesn't pan out?"

"Well, goddamn, have some faith, baby brother."

"I do, sis. I'm just saying is all."

Eureka nodded, "I feel you."

"What we got to drink?"

She rifled through a bag and pulled out two can sodas, holding them up.

"Do you want Pepsi or Dr. Pepper?"

"Pepsi."

She handed Anton the Pepsi and cracked open the Dr. Pepper. As she drunk the Dr. Pepper, she dipped her hand inside of her pocket and pulled out a receipt from Reggie's Liquor Store and Junior Market. It was the same receipt Fear had written his name and address on. Eureka was glad that she'd thought to bring it along because now she could pay him back once she sold the keys tomorrow. She folded the paper and stuck it back into her pocket.

The rest of the night she and Anton talked until he fell asleep. Eureka tucked a backpack under his head and draped his jacket over him. She kissed his head and settled in the driver's seat, tucking her Glock under her shirt. Laying her head back against the headrest she thought of a happier place and time. By the time sleep took her, she was wearing a smirk on her lips.

*****

The Next Morning...

Thud!

Something solid hit the car and caused it to rock, shaking Anton from his sleep. His head shot up from the backseat. He snapped from left to right trying to see what was going on. His eyes settled on a few men playing football in the middle of the street.

"That's game," one of them announced.

"Run that shit back," another one said.

Anton sighed. The man bumping up against the car scared the shit out of him. He thought Malvo and his goons had found their asses.

"Sis, you wouldn't believe who I thought it was when dude bumped up against the car." When he didn't hear a response from Eureka, a line formed across his forehead. He looked into the front seat and she was gone. Anton scratched the side of his face as he thought about where Eureka may have gone. Thirsty, he cracked open another can of Pepsi and guzzled it. He then polished off the last of the spicy Doritos that were in the bag, turning the bag up to get the crumbs that were left.

Anton took the keys out of the ignition and slid out of the car, brushing the crumbs from off his person. He gave a quick scan of the area before starting off to find Eureka. He'd gotten to the end of the block when he saw her coming across the other side of Figueroa. She had a greasy brown paper bag in one hand and a tray containing two sodas. He looked ahead and assumed that she must have just left Tom's Burger's on the corner of Florence and Figueroa. When she made it across the other side of Figueroa, he took the greasy brown paper bag from her.

"Man, I thought somebody had probably snatched you up," he said as they walked side by side, heading back toward the car.

"Nah, I figured I'd get us something hot to eat this morning," Eureka replied. "Those microwave burritos were not the business."

"As hungry as I was, that shit was as good as a short rib dinner from Bertha's," Anton confessed. "I couldn't get the wrapper off fast enough. A nigga was starving like a hostage last night."

"Baby boy, you're something else."

"What chu get me?" Anton rummaged through the greasy brown paper bag.

"Oh shit!" Eureka eyes almost popped out of her head and her mouth flew open. She dropped the tray of sodas and they exploded, spilling Hi-C fruit punch and Country Time Lemonade everywhere. She took off down the cracked sidewalk running as fast as she could. He looked up and saw a man hooking the Honda station wagon up to a tow truck. He dropped the greasy brown paper bag and took off after her. Together, they ran after the tow truck as it pulled off.

"Hold up! Stop!" Anton screamed.

"Wait, wait a minute!" Eureka screamed so loud that the veins in her neck bulged.

The harder they ran the further it seemed the tow truck was getting away. They ran until their chests were on fire and their legs were burning. Exhausted, they finally stopped. They stood beside one another watching the tow truck merge into traffic on Vermont Avenue. Eureka's eyes misted and hot tears trickled down her cheeks. She swiped them away with the back of her hand and looked at the street sign. There was no parking from 8 AM to 10 AM on Tuesdays.

Eureka grabbed a hold of the pole of the street sign and hung her head. Her body shook uncontrollably as she sobbed, big tears falling from her eyes and hitting the dirt patched sidewalk. Anton approached her and she wrapped her arms around him, sobbing into his shirt. He closed his eyes and caressed her back, comforting her. Their clothes, shoes, hygiene products, and most importantly the three blocks of cocaine they'd stolen was inside of that car. Without that to sling to get money, they were dead out in the streets. The only money they had was the few dollars she had in her pocket.

*****

They stayed at cheap motels over the next four days. On the fourth day she checked her finances and saw that she had twenty five dollars left. That was enough to buy her and Anton something to eat and still have a couple of bucks to spare. But after that she hadn't a clue of where they were going to lay their heads.

They ate inside of Burger King on the corner of King and Western. Eureka excused herself from the table and headed into the women's restroom. Once she relieved her bladder, she wiped herself and flushed the toilet. Pushing open the door of the stall, she approached the sink and washed her hands. After she dried her hands, she pulled out the last of her money and counted it. She shook her head shamefully seeing that she had eight funky ass dollars to her name. Eureka went to shove the money back into her pocket and spotted the receipt with Fear's number at her feet.

Staring at the digits of his telephone number she thought seriously about calling him, but her pride wouldn't allow her to seek refuge from anyone. She was taught to get it on her own. All she needed were her wits and her able body and she'd be straight.

Besides, she and Anton were strangers. What was the chance of him letting them crash at his spot for a time? Eureka balled up the receipt as she headed for the door, dropping it into the trash can. She made her way out of the women's restroom and headed back to the table. When she came around the corner she saw Anton struggling to stay awake as he kept nodding off to sleep. The manager came over to his table and said something to him. Anton nodded and the manager went about his duties.

Seeing this made Eureka understand that she had to put her own selfish needs aside and prioritize their needs for her brother's sake. She was his guardian and he was her responsibility. She had to do whatever she had to do in order to take care of him.

An epiphany struck Eureka like a closed fist and she darted back to the women's restroom. Plowing through the door, she snatched up the trash can and dumped its contents out on the center of the floor. She got down on her knees and rifled through all of the trash, looking for the receipt. She'd grown tired and was about to call it quits until fate smiled at her. A smile stretched across her face as she un-balled a slip of paper and discovered that she had the receipt. She held the receipt up in the air like Willie Wanka held up his golden ticket to The Chocolate Factory. Getting to her feet, Eureka left the women's restroom and stopped to holler at Anton.

"I've gotta make a call, I'll be right back," she told him, garnering a nod before she stepped out into the cool air of the night. She found a telephone booth just outside of Burger King. She snatched up the telephone and dropped thirty-five cents into the slot. She cradled the telephone to her ear with her shoulder, and punched in the number as she read them off of the receipt. Eureka looked about as the telephone ring, tapping her foot anxiously. She didn't know what she was going to say to him or how he'd react to her asking but she had to see what was up. He was her only hope. If he turned her down then she was stuck.

"Yooooo," Fear picked up on the third ring.

Eureka stood up straight and gripped the telephone tighter, pressing it to her ear. She tried to say something but the words got caught in her throat.

"Hello?"

Silence.

"Hellooo," Fear repeated.

He disconnected the call. Eureka hung up the telephone but kept a firm grip on the receiver. Closing her eyes, she bowed her head and took deep breaths. Inside of her head she went over some dialogue to say for when she called him back. When she moved to pick the telephone back up it rang and vibrated in her hand. Her brow furrowed. Wondering if it was him, she decided to answer it. She took the telephone from off of the hook and brought it to her ear slowly. Resting the telephone to her ear, she waited a few moments and then spoke.

"Hello?" she spoke timidly.

"Yeah, did someone just call here?"

"Yeah, sorry about that, it must have been a glitch in the line or something." she lied. "Listen, I don't know if you

139

remember me or not but you met me and my baby brother at Reggie's not too long ago."

"I remember y'all, Eureka and Anton," he recalled jovially. "Look, if you're calling me back to repay me, I'm not studying it. You gone and keep that, lil' momma. Like I told you before we're straight."

"Nah, nothing like that," she assured. "I've got myself in a jam and I need your help."

"What's up?" He'd suddenly grown serious.

Eureka exhaled, "Alright. Here goes."

She told him everything that occurred over the last few days. The only thing she left out were the murders and the three keys that they'd stolen from them. She had dropped thirty-five cents into the coin slot three more times to keep the line from disconnecting. But it was well worth it because once she'd given her report to Fear she felt relieved like a thousand pound weight had been lifted off of her shoulders and she was now as light as a feather.

"Gimmie like thirty minutes and I'll be down there to scoop y'all up."

"Alright," she replied, a smile emerging on her face. "And thank you."

"You're welcome lil' momma, y'all sit tight."

Eureka disconnected the call and turned around to Anton, who was sitting on the bus-stop crunching on the ice of his fountain drink.

"Who was that?"

"Fear."

"What chu want with him?"

"I asked him could we crash at his spot.

"What did he say?"

"We in there," she nodded her head. "He'll be here to pick us up in thirty minutes."

"Cool," Anton smiled and continued to crunch on his ice. Eureka sat beside him and laid her head up against his

140

shoulder. Now she had some place to lay her head for the time being until she figured out her next move.

Thank you, Daddy, she thought. Assuming that it was her father who had sent Fear to her and Anton's rescue.

Chapter 14

"Come on," Fear said over his shoulder to Eureka and Anton as he came through the door of his Paramount home. It was a nice two story, four bedroom, two bathroom house with a basement that Fear had modified into a Man Cave.

The house was located on a peaceful block that was inhabited by mostly Latino and African American families. She took in the living room as she followed Fear's lead. A 100" 3D flat-screen was mounted on the wall. The living room was uniquely decorated. A tribal spear, masks and portraits of African warriors and goddesses lined the walls. A statue of an African king sitting in his throne was in one corner of the room while a statue of an African queen was in the other. Both of the statues looked lifelike as if they would talk and walk around at any given moment. A zebra skin rug lay upon the floor with a black tinted glass table sitting on top of it. A black suede sectional sofa took up nearly all of the space inside of the living room.

"It's hot in here." Anton complained, wiping the sheen from his forehead.

"What you got the heat on? Hell?" Eureka fanned herself.

"Yeah, it is kind of hot." Fear agreed before adjusting the temperature dial on the heater. "Constance," he called out.

Moments later she emerged from the bedroom, moving down the hallway fluidly. The dimness of the corridor seemed to hide her face but left the rest of her visible. Eureka peered closely as she advanced. Her eyes seemed like glowing red orbs. Her thin dread locks were sprawled lazily over her face and shoulders, bouncing with every step that she took. She appeared to be moving theatrically in slow motion. Her garbs were a red tank top, red skinny jeans and Timberland boots. Her red fingernails looked like they had taken the form of talons. All of this coupled with the lingering heat made Constance resemble *the devil* walking on the burning surface of his domain—hell.

Eureka blinked her eyes and shook her head trying to gather her wits. Her eyes readjusted and she appeared normal. Constance stopped at the opening of the hallway and folded her arms across her chest. Lines formed diagonally on her forehead, her nose scrunched up and her lips twisted as if she smelled something foul. She sized Eureka up, looking upon her like she was a mannequin sculpted out of shit.

"Why you got the heat cranked up so high?" Fear pulled off his hoodie and slung it over his shoulder. "A nigga damn near passed out in here."

"Please, it's not even that hot in here, pull ya panties up, nigga."

"Whatever." He turned to them, making the introductions. "Eureka and Anton this is Constance. Constance this is Eureka and Anton."

"Hey," Eureka spoke.

"Watts up?" Anton threw his head back.

"Cat got cha tongue?" Fear asked her since she didn't speak.

Constance didn't utter a word. She and Eureka were engaged in a staring match.

Fear looked at them both. He could feel the tension in the air already.

"Constance, my guests spoke to you. You can't say *hi*?"

She rolled her eyes and exhaled as if speaking to them was going to hurt. She quickly threw up a fraudulent smile and said, "Hi, how're you doing?" she asked, sounding real preppy and proper.

Eureka didn't say shit. She's just met Constance and already she wasn't feeling her.

"I'ma hunnit," Anton mumbled like he didn't feel like talking. He didn't like her any more than Eureka did. The youngster was fiercely loyal to his sister. If you didn't fuck with her, then he didn't fuck with you. Besides, Constance made it easy not to like her.

Fear turned to his guests, rubbing his hands together. "Can I interest y'all in something to eat or drink?"

"Nah, we've already eaten," Eureka told him. "We would like to see where we'd be sleeping now, though."

"Cool," Fear turned to Constance, placing a hand on the lower part of her back. "Show them to their rooms for me. I gotta make a quick run."

Constance turned around and that bubble of hers was protruding in those red skinny jeans. Fear licked his lips and smacked her ass.

"Don't touch me!" she snapped.

He frowned, "Fuck is wrong with you?"

"We'll talk later."

"Go ahead, Ant. I'll catch up," Eureka told her baby brother. She watched him start after Constance before she stepped to Fear. "Thanks again." Eureka abruptly hugged him, holding onto him for a time before kissing his cheek. She was so grateful that he welcomed her and Anton into his home. He had spared her a great deal of hardship. Fear was taken off guard by Eureka's sudden act of appreciation. Reluctantly, he threw an arm around her and gently rubbed her back.

"Don't mention it, lil' momma."

Seeing the tender moment from over her shoulder as she led Anton to their bedroom caused Constance's face to contort with anger. Her top lip twitched with hatred and she gritted her teeth. She was only upset at first but now she was hot seeing his hand near the beginning of Eureka's protruding ass as he rubbed her back. Although, the small display of affection was innocent, she saw it as a major violation. Initially, she had only saw Eureka as a potential threat to what she and Fear had when she entered the house, but now she saw her as a force to be reckoned with.

She hurried along to catch up with Constance and Anton as they went up with the staircase.

******

"This is you." Constance opened the door of the bedroom.

Eureka stuck her head inside. It had a warm feel to it. It was decorated in chocolate brown, rust brown and gold. There was a canopy bed that looked like it came out of the 18th century. The dressers and nightstand had an antique look as well. The furniture was made to look worn. The craftsman wanted it to look shabby and haggard yet sophisticated and stylish. Out of all of the bedrooms in the house Constance loved this one the most because she'd decorated it herself.

"Your bedroom is right across the hall," Constance pointed.

"Nah," Eureka shook her head. "We'll hole up in here together."

"Suit yourself."

"I gotta use the bathroom," Anton announced.

"Down the hall, to the left." Constance had her eyes super glued to Eureka.

"I'll be right back, sis. You good?" he asked, noticing she and Constance were locked into one another's gazes.

"Yeah, baby boy, go ahead." Eureka answered, keeping her eyes on her.

Once Anton had left, Constance took a step back and closed the door shut without breaking eye contact with Eureka. Constance locked the door and stepped to her. When she did this, Eureka hooked her thumb in the belt loop of her jeans. Her Glock was at the small of her back and if Constance tried her she was going to push her wig back.

The Devil Wears Timbs

"Let me tell you something. That nigga in there is mines, all mines. He's spoken for. So, if you know what's good for you you'll keep yo lil' young ass up outta his face," Constance threatened.

Eureka looked her up and down like she'd lost her goddamn mind. If it wasn't for her and Anton needing a place to crash, she would have uprooted her banger and cracked Constance's egg until the yoke spilt out that mothafucka.

"Is that a threat?"

"Yes, bitch." Constance punched her palm for emphasis. "It is a threat! I'm telling you right now. If you don't stay the fuck away from my dude, then I'm gonna plant cho ass inside of a fucking hole in the ground. You and yo lil' punk ass brotha. If you're looking for an issue, I'm that bitch!" she smacked herself across the chest as spittle jumped from her lips, sprinkling Eureka's nose. "You've been warned." She twisted her lips and looked Eureka up and down like she wasn't shit. She then pulled open the door and turned back around. She made her hand into the shape of a gun and pointed it at Eureka, mimicking the sounds of a gun firing, *"Pow! Pow!"* Constance blew imaginary smoke from the tip of her finger and turned around, bumping shoulders with Anton as she came out into the hallway.

"Bitch," he said under his breath as he stepped into the bedroom.

Eureka stood there staring into space. Her face was balled up with anger and veins formed in her forehead and neck. Her nostrils flared and she clenched her jaws tightly, flexing the muscles in her face. She was so hot that you'd get a third degree burn from touching her. Fist balled, jaws tightened, Eureka looked like she was about ready to explode like a stick of dynamite. Finally, she hung her head and took deep breaths to calm herself. It took everything she had to stop from A-Town stomping Constance into the floor.

146

"You okay, sis?" That broad didn't do anything to you, did she?"

"Nah, I'm gucci." Eureka brought her head up and smiled, patting him on the back.

"You sure? 'Cause if it's a problem, you and me can burn this mothafucka to the ground."

"Look at chu, always ready to ride for your big sis." She playfully punched him in the shoulder.

"You know how we do. Fuck with one of us, you fuck with both of us," Anton stated wholeheartedly.

"As bad as I'd love to ride out on that bitch, we can't afford to fuck up our stay here right now," Eureka told him. "We need to marinate here until I figure out our next move."

Anton nodded his understanding. "I was thinking on our way over here. Why don't we just stick with what we started?"

Eureka plopped down on the bed and exhaled saying, "I don't know, Ant. I mean…"

"Come on now, sis, we had three blocks of raw," Anton said excitedly. "Imagine if we would have slung them white bitches for fifteen grand a pop. That's forty-five racks, all profit. Tell me you wouldn't have loved that," he plopped down on the bed beside her, smiling from ear to ear. He watched as Eureka struggled to contain her smile but eventually lost. "See," he hopped off the bed, swinging on the air. "That's what I'm talking about. You feel me? Now, imagine if we were hitting fools for that much or more two, three times a night. We'd come off like a fat kid in a pastry shop."

"I hear you, baby brother," Eureka responded. "The money is sweet, but the risks…" she shook her head knowing that the game wasn't anything nice. Things could have gone left that night when they pulled that kick door, but luck was on their side. Next time things could go south and either one of them could end up stretched out with a hole in them. Eureka figured that she would take her wins where she could get them. In the game Anton wanted to play, you had to be all in.

"Tell me you didn't get a thrill," Anton said. "I mean, standing their gripping that cannon and mothafuckaz doing whatever you tell 'em 'cause they know you hold their life or death in your hand—that shit gets your adrenalin pumping. It's a high like no other. I felt it and I know you did too. I could tell. It was plastered all over your face."

Eureka couldn't front. He was right. She loved the thrill she got from kicking in doors and making fuck-niggaz lay it down. It was something about it that made her kitty cat tingle and moisten. Eureka was only five feet, five inches and weighed one hundred and twenty pounds but when that burner was in her hand she felt like she was six foot tall, with a hefty weight of two hundred and fifty on her. She'd never felt alive until she busted her first jack move. She was exhilarated when she took a nigga'z shit. She was for sure she wouldn't get that same feeling busting her hump for minimum wage at some dead end job.

"Alright, I'ma keep it a buck," she began. "I got my shits and giggles out of it. But that shit there is real, lil' brother. It's not for play, play. There are some serious repercussions that come behind that. You should expect death, jail, and/or a life time of looking over your shoulder. If you can accept that, then and only then should you play in that game, ya feel me?"

"Sis, we're from the projects. "Death, jail, and a lifetime of looking over your shoulder are already in the cards."

"True dat," Eureka nodded. "We'll continue this conversation another day. Right now, I'm tryna catch some Z's."

She slid her steel protector underneath her pillow. She then slipped her feet out of her Timbs and slid in the bed, under the covers.

"Alright," Anton untied his sneakers and pulled them off. He slid in at the foot of the bed under the covers.

Eureka killed the lamp light and snuggled back under the covers.

"I love you, stupid."

"I love you more, sis." He closed his eyes for a good night's rest.

*****

Constance sat Indian-style on the bed with a tray lying on her lap. A razor, a small pile of Kush and a packet of grape Swisher Sweets were laying upon the tray. She went about the task of rolling the swisher with an expertise that could have only been developed from years of practice.

Constance licked the swisher closed. She then took a Bic and swept its flame back and forth across it, sealing it shut. She placed it between her thin lips and took a pull. She blew out a cloud of smoke just as Fear entered the bedroom.

He came in pulling his hoodie over his head and kicking off his Timbs. Once he'd stripped down to his Joe boxer- briefs, he plopped down on the bed and grabbed the remote control. Folding the pillow behind his head, he turned on the 50" flat-screen and flipped through the channels.

"We need to talk."

"About what?" Fear asked, keeping his eyes glued on the flat-screen.

"Fuck you think?" Constance frowned. "Those two kids you brought home. Where did they come from?"

"You know that thing I handled with ol' boy that was hustling on the wrong soil?" She nodded *yes*. "He was about to shoot 'em, but I bartered a deal and he let 'em go free."

"And?"

"Those two have been through a lot." Fear gave her the rundown on them and everything they'd been through in the past few days. "They just need a place to lay their heads for a time until they figure out what they're gonna do."

"And you thought it was cool to bring 'em here knowing the kind of business we're involved in?" She asked with her eyebrows raised, looking at him like 'You know that that shit wasn't smart'.

"After she'd told me what they'd been through there was no way that I could turn them down."

Constance shook her head as she stared at Fear, "You've gotten soft."

"I guess I was soft when I rescued your black ass from that brothel too, huh?"

"That was different."

"Oh, that was different?" he folded his arms across his chest. "Well, do explain how their situation and your situation were so different."

"Whatever, Alvin, it ain't that serious," she waved him off. "I'm really not in the mood to be going back and forth with you."

"Yeah, you can't find any merit, so that means I win *again*."

She took a few pulls from her L and blew smoke.

"You ain't won jack shit. I just don't feel like arguing all night with yo ass," she claimed. "Your lil' friends can stay tonight but come tomorrow morning I want 'em gone."

Fear turned off the TV with the remote control and sat up in bed, looking upon Constance with a frown.

"Hold up," he began, "You don't run notta goddamn thang here. This is my crib," he patted the bed. "I decided who stays and who goes."

"As long as I'm your woman, can't no other pussy lay up in here." As soon as the words left her lips, she wished she hadn't spoken them. Even though her mind knew they weren't an item, her heart believed otherwise.

Tranay Adams

Constance didn't mean to fall in love with Fear, but she did. It was something that just happened. She didn't even think that she could love with all of the shit she'd been through. She truly believed that she was incapable of such an emotion. But then Fear entered her life and rescued her from the nightmare that was her reality.

See, her father had given her to a pimp to pay a debt. She spent a number of years selling pussy on the streets before she was eventually stolen from him and forced to work as a sex slave. Having grown tired of the nightmare that was her life, Constance sliced open her wrists with a Gemstar razor as she lay in a tub of hot water. She was teetering between life and death when Fear came bursting through the door of the brothel, looking to recover some stolen whores for his client. Seeing as how she wasn't one of the girls on his repo list he started to leave her to die, but there was something at the back of his mind that told him to take her with him.

He brought Constance home like she was a stray dog that he found wandering the streets. He cleaned her up and nursed her back to health. For this, Constance felt that she was indebted to Fear. She pledged her life to him. Her mind, body and soul was his to do with as he pleased. But he declined the offer, reasoning that he'd done what he'd done because it felt right at the moment. Nonetheless, she insisted that he allow her to pay him back. Being in the kind of business that he was in, Fear realized that he would need someone playing his shadow to watch his back. Knowing this, he enlisted her and taught her everything she knew about the murder game.

Constance was inventive, clever, ruthless, callous and professional. She possessed all of the traits to make for the perfect killer. However, for all of her strengths she had one weakness, her love for Fear. She and he had spent so much time together that she couldn't help herself feeling besotted by him. She tried with all of her might to deny her feelings, but they wouldn't go away. She hated herself for having these

151

feelings and she took up time with other men to dissolute them. But it didn't work. She had already become obsessed with him. Constance Payne had a real life fatal attraction.

"Wait a minute. Rewind that shit. *Woman*?" Fear looked at her like '*You got to be kidding me.*' Me and you aren't an item. We work together and share a fuck every now and again. That's it."

"Oh, so it's like that now?"

"It's been like that," he reconfirmed. "I let you know what it was with me from the door so don't go acting like a nigga played you. We've gotta pretty good arrangement. But if you feel like it's getting too hectic for you, then we can keep it strictly business."

Fear could see the anger and pain in Constance's glassy eyes. For a woman so beautiful he couldn't understand how she could be so ugly. At times he found himself wondering was she really as cold as she portrayed or was she putting up a front because she was a woman and knew that such behavior wouldn't be expected?

Constance had proven her worth. She wasn't expendable. Chicks like her didn't come a dime a dozen. They came around every now and again like a solar eclipse. Fear had love for her, but he wasn't in love with her. There was a difference. He'd told her from the get go that he wasn't looking to get into a relationship. All he wanted was a goodtime and a friendly fuck every now and again. Though Constance had agreed to go with his program, he was reluctant in dealing with someone whom he worked with. He knew that even though she acted hard-body that she was still a woman underneath that rough exterior. Therefore, she was subjected to the same emotions like every woman was.

Fear had planned on smashing her once and keeping it moving, but the pussy was too good. He had to go back. He couldn't help himself. He couldn't keep his dick to himself. His having a *goodtime* and *friendly fucking* eventually lead to

152

Constance catching feelings. She began to believe their relationship could grow into more than what it was, ignoring what he had said before hand.

"Nah, we're good where we're at."

"Alright then, let this be the last time I have to tell you your place." Fear reached over and took the L that was pinched between her fingers. Taking puffs, he could see the anger and frustration in her face. "I see you're sitting on some steam over there. What's up? You need that?" He mashed out the L in the ashtray and gave Constance his undivided attention.

"I don't need nothing from a nigga that's *not* my man." He tried to touch her thigh and she swatted his hand. "Move, man, I ain't fucking with chu."

Her smacking his hand didn't stop him from trying her again. It was like his hand had a mind of its own as it traveled up the length of her thick succulent thigh. Her conscience told her to stop his hand as it took its tour of her body, but her sudden arousal betrayed her, allowing him to do as he pleased. Constance sucked on her bottom lip as she watched his hand, wishing she had the discipline to put up a fight.

Why this nigga always gotta fight dirty when we get into it? Knowing damn well a bitch can't resist his touch. Oh, my God, look at that fat juicy dick of his, umm, she shuddered and gasped for air, grasping the silk black sheets on the bed. Fear's dick was stirring awake inside of his boxers. Its movements was like those of a serpent. *That mothafucka looks like an anaconda tryna escape from a pillowcase.*

"I know you're sick, baby, and Daddy's got the antidote."

He licked Constance from her collarbone, up to her chin, nibbling and sucking under it. She tilted her head back and closed her eyes. Soft and sensuous moans escaped her lips, giving him the cue to keep going. He slipped his chocolate hand into her boy shorts and parted her sweet, delicate flower before slipping two of his fingers inside of her. Pressing his thumb against her clit, he rubbed it in circles as his fingers fucked her moist, pink hole.

She squirmed under his addictive touch, arching her back. She opened her legs wider for him to go deeper and he granted her wish, adding more fingers to the equation. Her eyes rolled back in her head and her mouth dropped open. Fear felt so good inside of her that she wanted to scream his name, but the sensation his fingers brought forth choked her up. Constance looked down at his hand and it was in her down to the knuckles.

She lifted her ass from off of the bed and grinded into his hand, matching its movements precisely. While his fingers worked their magic, he used his free hand to pull that black mamba of his out of hiding. That big swollen mothafucka stood at attention just like a King Cobra, ready to attack.

Fear took Constance's hand and guided it to his black steel. She grasped it and loved the feeling of it in her palm. As she stroked his meaty pole, he worked her middle, their hands moved with the same rhythm as if they were both dancing to the same music.

Once his dick was as hard as it was going to get, and she'd busted her second nut, he pulled his hand free. He brought it before his eyes and they both looked upon it admiringly. It was glistening and sticky with her juices. She grabbed him by the wrist and leaned his hands to her lips. Staring him dead in his eyes, she sucked her own juice from his fingers, one by one. Once Constance was done, Fear laid back on the bed. Lifting his back from off of the bed, he slipped off his boxers and flung them aside. He then helped her remove her boy shorts.

"What chu waiting for? Gone and saddle 'em up," he spoke of his dick. His shit was as hard as niggaz on a level four prison yard. Constance pulled open the dresser drawer, dipped her hand inside and came back up with a condom. She tore the golden foil wrapper open with her teeth and freed the lubricated latex from its confinement. She then placed the condom on the tip of his pole and rolled it down with both hands until she reached the stubble on his mound. Before climbing on top of him, she took a good look at his joint tilting her head to the side. His dick resembled one of those long rolls of salami hanging up inside of the refrigerator at a deli. She squatted over it and eased herself down onto it, until they became one.

Constance brow furrowed and she clenched her jaws. She could feel Fear stuffed between her slickened walls. She closed her eyes and bit down on her bottom lip. She threw her hips gently until her sex box produced enough juices for her to ride him comfortably. Once she was good and wet, she began rotating her hips vigorously. It started feeling good to her and she sunk her nails into his chest. She leaned forward allowing her dreads to dangle down in his face.

"I'ma make this dick mine. I'ma put my mothafucking name on it," she rasped. Constance blew her sweet, hot breath into his face as she threw that ass harder, faster, grinding into him.

Fear was buried so deep inside of her that she could feel him up in her stomach. Enjoying the feeling of her internal glove, he gripped her chunky ass and threw his head back. His eyelids fluttered as he licked his top lip in blissfulness. That pussy was wet, warm, tight and crafted perfectly to fit him perfectly.

"Ahhhh, shhhhit," Fear uttered, squeezing Constance's ass as she rode him like a wild bull at a rodeo.

He spanked her ass signaling her to ride him faster and aggressively. That rough shit turned her on. She loved thug passion. Fear didn't know what Constance had done to her pussy, but it was better than it had ever been before. That thang was insane and needed to be thrown in a strait jacket and shoved inside of a padded room.

The Devil Wears Timbs

"Goddamn, what the fuck?" He frowned, inhaling and exhaling like a woman during child birth. He could feel that baby batter stirring around inside of his balls and knew that it would soon rush to the head of his dick.

"Gon', baby, gon' and let momma get that nut up out chu," Beads of sweat oozed from out of the pores of her forehead and slowly started to cast down her brows. Constance stared down at the ugly faces Fear made as she rode him. He lifted his head from the pillow and brought his lips just below the name inked on her left breast. *Alvin.*

Fear sucked on that breast as if it was leaking fresh vanilla ice cream. When he was finished with the left breast, he went to the right giving them both an equal amount of attention. She pushed his back against the headboard and squatted on his fuck organ, placing her hands on his chest above the *Bout Dat Life* tattoo on his abs. He tried to take control of the situation, but she swatted his hand away.

"Uh uh," she shook her head, "I got this."

Constance started off at a normal pace but slowly sped up, sliding that round brown thang down his thick, chocolate pole. His eyes rolled to the white and his mouth dropped open as she put that pussy on him like only she could. She watched as he hissed and grunted, while she continued to drop that fat bodacious ass on him. She closed her eyes and licked her lips as she enjoyed the pleasure he brought her. Her thick white cream gushed out of her slick, pink hole and coated his steel, running down his bald nut-sack and seeping inside of his asshole.

"Who this big dick belong to?" Constance asked with a glistening body, looking down into his face which was a mask of ecstasy. When Fear didn't answer her she asked him again. Suddenly, his eyes peeled open and he looked up at her.

"This big mothafucka belongs to the nigga that it's attached to," he answered arrogantly. "Turn around and lay that ass across the bed," he smacked Constance on her ass and

156

she did exactly as he commanded. Fear got into a pushup like position with his fists pressed into the bed as he hovered above her. The head of his swollen fuck organ was pressed up against her left butt cheek, indenting it. Without using his hands, he drew his meaty pole back and slowly pushed it inside of her awaiting opening. It was his turn to act a dog ass fool up in that pussy.

He gave it to her hard and rough, slamming his meaty pole into her slopping moisture down to his public hairs. His shaved mound smacked up against her protruding ass creating what sounded like a pair of hands clapping at an opera.

Constance was throwing her ass back at first, and her movements were in sync with his until he found that G-spot of hers and exploited it for all it was worth. From there she collapsed on the bed and submitted to his stroke as he pushed her toward the doors of euphoria. Fear was showing that pussy who was boss, hitting the bottom of that mothafucka and causing a sloshing noise in its wetness. He was handling his like a Dick Slinging champion and her sex noises were proof of that.

"That's right, baby, gone and get that mothafucka off." Fear drilled her from above. "I know that's all you needed. Work got chu stressed, yo nigga not acting right. Shit ain't going how you want it to. Gone and get it, momma, this dick is yours tonight."

"Ahh! Ahh! Ahh!" Constance's voice went up octaves as she met each of Fear's powerful thrusts.

She pulled the silk black sheets into her as she bit down on a pillow, pleased by his third leg. Feeling her walls enclosing around his meat as he pushed and pulled himself in and out of her glory hole, he gritted his teeth and closed his eyes tightly. Fighting back the urge to explode and flood the latex glove. His tenseness showed on his face through its turning red and the veins forming on his neck. Constance's pussy was tight. It felt like a hand was wrapped around his meaty pole as he threw it in and out of her grip. Realizing that he couldn't hold back anymore, Fear snatched himself out of her, pulled off the condom, and stroked until his head oozed with his secret sauce. White droplets rained down upon her ass cheeks as she shook them and smiled over her shoulder.

"Woooo, that pussy is the truth." Fear cracked a smile and smacked her ass cheek, causing it to jiggle like a bowl of Jell-O. Using his index finger, he signed his name in the secret sauce he'd soiled her ass cheek with. It read: *Fear*. "I had to give it that official stamp."

Constance propped her head upon her fist and watched as he walked his naked ass into the bathroom to take a shower. A smile etched her face. She was madly in love and she'd murder anyone that tried to get in the way of it, including Eureka. Constance's face morphed into a scowl and a pair of sneering lips as she looked to the door, thinking about her. She was good just as long as she stayed out of his face but if she tried anything slick, there would be a lot of slow singing and flower bringing. Word to Biggie.

Chapter 15

"Good morning." Fear greeted Eureka and Anton as he entered the kitchen. He was clad in a red doo-rag and matching silk pajama pants that hung low in the front, boasting that V that lead to the stubble of his mound.

"Good morning," she threw up a smile from where she sat on the sofa.

"Top of the AM, my nigga," Anton replied. "I hope you don't mind." He held up the bowl of Captain Crunch he was eating.

"Nah, help yourself, family." He moved about the kitchen, preparing a mug of coffee. "Mi casa su casa," he looked to Eureka holding up a mug. "You want some coffee?"

"Sure," she nodded.

"How do you like it?"

"Cream, sugar, you know. The regular."

"Got it," he tossed the mug around his back and caught it at his front.

"Soooo, somebody got 'em some last night, huh?" Eureka analyzed.

Fear chuckled and said, "Is it that obvious, lil' momma?"

"I would say," she said, "You gotta lil' pep to your step this morning."

"Yeah, I got right."

"That's what's up." She looked around for Constance. "So, uh, where's your girlfriend?"

"Girlfriend? Sheeiit, I can't remember the last time I had one of those," Fear confessed.

"She told me that y'all were an item."

"Oh, really?" he asked with a raised eyebrow.

"Yep, said that you were her booski. Thank you." Eureka took the cup from him as he passed it to her and sat down on the sofa.

"Nah." He picked a piece of lent off of his pants and brushed it off.

"Soooo, uh, what exactly is she to you then?" She grinned as she sipped from the mug.

"Why do you wanna know?" he shot her a million dollar smile.

"Different reasons," Eureka fired back with a million dollar smile of her own.

Fear hunched forward, gripping the mug with both hands. He gave it some thought, "Constance is my confidant, my friend, and my family. I'd kill for her and I'd die for her. Vice versa."

"Respect," Eureka smirked. "I feel the same about that knucklehead." She casted her eyes in Anton's direction. He was inside of the kitchen washing out his bowl and spoon. "Look." She turned her neck so Fear could see the name tattooed on her neck in stylish lettering, *Anton*.

"Y'all tight, huh?" he asked.

"Yeah, that's my nigga right there." Eureka smiled at her baby brother lovingly.

"Watts up?" Anton asked as he returned to the living room. He hadn't a clue of what they were talking about. She shook her head like *'Nothing.'*

"Listen." Fear sat his mug down on the coffee table. "Why don't y'all go and get ready. I'ma take y'all shopping today."

Her forehead wrinkled at the thought of him spending money on them. She sat up on the sofa and sat her mug on the coffee table. "I appreciate the offer, but I've already told you that we..." she was cut short by him throwing up a hand.

"I know. You don't accept charity." Fear interrupted, repeating what Eureka had said when they'd first met. "And

160

Tranay Adams

this is not what this is. You're paying me back. What chu owe me, forty-seven dollars and some change from that day at Reggie's?" she nodded. "Okay then, I'll add this lil' shopping spree to your tab. Cool?" He pointed to her and she nodded. He pointed to Anton and he nodded. "Alright then, y'all go get ready. I'ma warm up this coffee." He picked up the mug and rose to his feet.

"Alright, but I'm paying you back." she reiterated.

"Aye, that's the deal." He extended his hand and she shook it.

"Come on, Ant. Let's go get ready." Eureka threw her arm over her baby brother's shoulders and they headed for the staircase.

As they neared the top of the staircase they saw Constance stroll across their line of vision with her silk robe rippling in the air behind her. Underneath the robe she was as naked as the day she was born. You could see her plentiful breasts and her scrumptious body. Constance had a physique that was made for the cover of a swimsuit magazine. She rolled her eyes at Eureka and twisted her lips as she kept it moving, toting a clear bottle of Johnson and Johnson's baby oil. With each step she took that bodacious ass of hers jumped one cheek at a time. Anton's eyes bulged and his mouth dropped open as he ogled her. Eureka smacked a hand over his eyes but he quickly snatched it down, observing Constance until she'd vanished out of his sight.

"I don't like that broad, but goddamn her body make a young nigga wanna wash her car and mow the lawn, sheesh."

Eureka laughed and continued up the stairs with Anton tucked under her arm. She couldn't help but think, *If this bitch thinks she's jelly now, I'ma have her hating the ground that I walk on by the end of the day.*

Constance entered the bedroom not even bothering to close the door shut. She allowed the silk house robe to fall to the floor on her way to the bed. Plopping down on the bed, she

161

poured baby oil into her palm and began rubbing her arms and legs down. Fear came into the bedroom, closing the door shut behind him. A line formed on his forehead as he moved to the closet, rifling through the clothes for something to wear for the day.

"Damn, ma, you left the door open while you're in here naked and shit. You know I got guests."

"Fuck yo' guests."

"What?"

"You heard me, nigga." Constance rose from the bed and approached him. The baby oil made her beautiful body shine like wet leather under the light. Her double d's slightly jiggled with each step that she took toward him. Fear suddenly became hypnotized by her body. His eyebrows raised and his mouth dropped open with shock and arousal. His eyes traveled up from her shaved fat pussy to the cinnamon brown melons sitting on her chest. Fear could hear them begging to be groped and fondled with, and he eagerly wanted to oblige them.

Constance pushed his chin up with her finger so that he'd be looking into her eyes. "If you want me to shut up, why don't you put something in my mouth and make me?" she said seductively, nibbling and sucking on the soft flesh under his chin.

Fear tilted his head back and hissed. His dick rocked up inside of his pajama pants, standing long and hard. That big black bastard was so sturdy that you could do pull-ups and dips on it. Constance continued sucking on the soft flesh under his chin as she tugged on his meaty pole and caused pre-cum to ooze out of its head. She got down on her knees and pulled his pajama pants down around his ankles. She then used her thumb to rub the pre-cum in around the head. She lifted his package up so that she'd be facing its nut sack. Dipping her head low, she stuck her tongue inside of his asshole. As soon as Fear felt the warm, wetness of her tongue, he clenched his buttocks and rose to the tips of his toes.

Constance dragged her long tongue from his asshole and stalled at the line that separated his sack. She sucked on his left nut as if it were a deviled egg and drew soft moans from his lips. She moved to the right nut and gave it the exact same treatment.

Once she was done pampering the twins, her tongue traveled the length of his hard-on and stopped at the head of it. She allowed it to rest on her tongue for a time before taking it inside of her mouth. She whipped her lips up and down that mothafucka, spilling her saliva down its length. Slowly, Constance brought her head down the meaty pole, taking it in every couple of inches. She gagged a little during the transition, but eventually she made it all of the way down to the stubble of Fear's mound. She stopped here for a couple of seconds, letting him rest inside of the hot, slickened tunnel that was her throat.

Looking up at him, she could tell from the expression on his face that he loved every minute of her head game. Seeing him pleased caused her nipples to stiffen and her pretty kitty to run like a faucet with her juices. Constance pulled back regurgitating Fear inch by inch until his entire endowment was visible.

Constance wiped her mouth with the back of her fist. She stared at his glistening endowment as she held it in her hand. Suddenly, she scowled, pursed her lips and spat on it twice, totally disrespecting the dick as if she couldn't stand it. Two lengths of saliva hung deathly close to the floor from his dick. She used her tongue to catch the first and bring it back over to his shaft. She did the same to the second.

She grabbed the dick with both hands. Using both of her hands, she stroked it vigorously while staring up into his face. Constance head game was so vicious that it caused his knees to buckle. He had to keep one hand pressed against the wall to stop from falling out. Fear's eyes narrowed and his mouth dropped open as she tugged on his dick. He was so choked up by the glorious sensation that all he could do was groan like a walking dead man.

"Hold on," Fear said, taking his hand away from the wall. He laid his steel between her breasts and told her to mash them bitches together. He then gripped both of her oiled shoulders and locked eyes with her as he slowly began to titty fuck her. He grunted with every stroke, going faster with each and every thrust. Those big ass titties were just as good as a tight, wet pussy. Holding his gaze, Constance licked her long tongue out at him enticing him to cum. This rallied him up and he sped up a notch, hitting the tip of her tongue with each of his strokes. "You sexy, fine, freak motahfucka you!" he rasped out of breath. "You wanna nigga to bust off don't you? You wanna nigga to bust off on them big gigantic ass titties, huh?" She nodded as she stared up at his creased forehead and scrunched nose. He squeezed her shoulders tighter and pumped between her titties aggressively, causing her to tilt back and damn near fall. Fear bit down on his bottom lip as he whined and continued to stroke like a man possessed by an evil nympho spirit. "Ah, damn! Ooooh, shit! I'ma 'bout to come."

"There you go, Daddy. Make that big mothafucka come. Bust off on these big juicy ass titties," she urged him, hungry to receive his own personal ranch dressing.

"Ooooh, fuck, fuck." Fear's face creased and scrunched up so tight that he looked like another nigga. Quickly, he snatched himself from between Constance's titties and squeezed it tightly at the head so that he wouldn't release too soon. "Squeeze them mothafuckaz together and hold 'em up. Keep ya tongue out too, goddamn it."

She squeezed her titties together and kept her tongue out just like he'd ordered. "Here you go. Ahhhhh!" His dick came up spitting like an Uzi. He tatted up Constance's titties, mouth, lips and face with his warm liquid. The nigga damn near blinded the bitch from shooting off so hard. Fear stroked his steel making sure that he'd gotten out every last drop of cum. He then scooped up some of his cum off of her chest and brought it toward her lips. She grabbed him by the wrist and sucked his finger clean, licking it one last time. "That was the lick right there. Good looking out." He smacked Constance on the ass as she picked up her silk house robe and sauntered off to the bathroom adjoined to the bedroom. Once she closed the door shut behind her, his shoulders slacked and he collapsed onto the bed, exhaustedly. He wiped the beads of sweat from his forehead with the back of his hand as he breathed heavily. A smile graced his face as he thought about how good a shot of head Constance had.

"Goddamn," Fear said. "Head of Legends out this muthafucka." He looked to the bathroom door yelling, "Yo', Constance, hurry up, I gotta piss like a race horse." He crawled across the bed and grabbed his pack of smokes from off of the nightstand. He withdrew a square and fired it up, expelling smoke from his nostrils and grill.

*****

Constance cleaned herself up and tossed the soiled towel onto the commode. She then brushed her teeth and tongue, thoroughly. Constance knew she had some fool ass head and some pussy niggaz would get into a shootout over.

She blessed Fear with one of her superior talents in hopes that he'd think twice before kicking her to the curb to take up time with the next bitch. She just hoped that it was enough for the time being because if not a candle light visual and mural was going to be getting setup on somebody's block real soon. Where good head and pussy had failed she was sure a .45 automatic and hollow point bullets would prevail.

She wasn't really trying to go there because she wasn't trying to get into it with Fear over her snuffing Eureka's flame

The Devil Wears Timbs

out but fuck it, eventually he would get over it, like he'd gotten over the others.

Constance twisted the dials and turned the faucet's water off. She then patted her mouth dry, threw the silk house robe back on and headed out of the bathroom. She didn't know how things would play out with her and Eureka living under the same roof, but she was sure of one thing. She'd smoke her ass before she let her steal Fear's heart.

*****

Fear took them to Downtown Los Angeles off of Maple and 11th Avenue. Downtown was a place where you could find deals on just about anything that you could think of and more. They had everything a department store would have only it would be cheaper which was why it was always crowded down there. You would have thought that there was a parade happening every day considering the vast amount of people that roamed throughout the street looking for whatever their hearts desired for a bargain.

They tore the stores up. Fear paid for whatever they wanted. They had so many bags of clothes and shoes that they had to make two trips to the car before they could finish shopping. Eureka made sure to keep the receipts from every store that they purchased something from because she was going to make sure that she paid him back.

After scoffing down hotdogs wrapped in bacon and topped with the works, they polished off their drinks and dropped them into the gated trash cans aligning the streets. Fear sent Anton off to cop him a couple of leather belts and Pro-clubs while he, Eureka, and Constance ducked off inside of a women's boutique on the corner of 11th Avenue. The store was about as big as a Boost Mobile store and was loaded with clothes racks from the ceiling to the floor. There were also clothes racks scattered throughout the floor.

Fear sat in a chair watching Eureka try on clothes. He gave her either a thumb-up or a thumb-down depending on whether he liked her ensemble or not. Every few minutes she was in and out of the dressing room with a dress for Fear to critique. Any other man would have been ready to leave after having been downtown all of that time shopping, but he was actually enjoying himself. Shooting the breeze with her, he came to the realization that she was a real down to earth chick. She liked everything that men liked except for pussy.

Eureka liked sports, beer, gambling, and the occasional blunt. It was safe to say that kicking it with her was like passing time with one of the fellas. On top of that, she had a body to die and come back alive for. Fear was pleasantly surprised, too. He was expecting her to be built like a ten year old boy given how petite she was, but underneath all of those baggy clothes she was quite shapely with a juicy, fat ass that you'd want to hug and snuggle your face up against. With personality and good looks Eureka was the total package. All he needed to know was if she was 'bout it when it came to holding a nigga down if he opted to court her.

Anton returned to the boutique with a bag containing the items that Fear sent him out for and his change from the purchases. Once he'd given Fear his change and the bag, he headed back out to find these certain pair of Air Jordan's that he was looking for. On his way out he brushed shoulders with Constance, who was toward the entrance of the store pretending to be searching through the clothes racks. For a time she had been spying on their interaction with one another. Through her observation she'd gathered that he was somewhat feeling her which really got the water inside of her pot boiling. It was like she was intentionally trying to get under Constance's skin.

Eureka emerged from the dressing room wearing a sleeveless, low cut white blouse with ruffling and a charcoal gray pencil dress. Out of the corner of her eye she could see

Constance laying in the cut acting like she was looking through the clothes racks when she already had nearly every item inside of the store waiting for her on the counter.

Look at this broad, uptight than a muthafucka. Scared somebody gon' snatch this nigga. I know the past couple of hours down here must have been hell for that ass 'cause I've been fucking with her head tough. If she thinks she's heated now, wait until she peep this next move.

"What do you think of this one?" Eureka smiled, as she did a three hundred and sixty degree turn for Fear to take a good look at what she was wearing.

"You did that," Fear nodded, liking how the ensemble looked on her. It hugged her curves like Saran wrap and had her ass on poked out. How could he disagree with her rocking it? Sheeiiit, he'd be a fool to.

"Cool. I'ma get this and we can get up outta here." Eureka tried to unzip the pencil skirt at the back but its zipper wouldn't budge. She tugged on it a couple of times but it still wouldn't come undone. "I can't get this zipper to budge. You mind giving it a try?"

"Alright." Fear attempted to help, but she grabbed his wrist.

"Hold on," Eureka stopped him. "Let's go inside of the dressing room, may be some pervs out here."

As she led him toward the dressing room, she glanced over her shoulder and smiled deviously at Constance.

Constance was flame broiling Whopper grill hot. Her eyes glazed over and she grinded her teeth so hard that she could literally hear them grinding against each other. She was about 5.5 seconds from snatching that .45 automatic from out of her purse, kicking open that dressing room door and giving Eureka a bad case of lead poisoning.

Calm down now, calm down, she thought to herself as she bowed her head and massaged the bridge of her nose. *This is not the place to catch a body. There are too many people*

168

out here. Besides, that gutta snipe hoe ain't trying to do nothing but get a reaction out of you. Take it easy. Breathe, momma. Breathe. That's it. Constance began to wind down as she held council inside of her head. Her breathing came to a normalcy with slow, steady breaths. Finally, she took one last deep breath and relieved herself of all of the rage that had swelled inside of her chest.

When she looked up, Eureka was walking up to the counter with the clothes she planned on purchasing while Fear lagged behind talking on his cell phone. They locked eyes. While Constance gave her the look of death, Eureka just looked at her with a smile like, *Hahahaha, you mad, bitch?*

Constance wanted to sink her nails where Eureka's forehead began and yank it down, stripping the skin from off of her face. Instead, she decided to come at her in another fashion altogether. As Eureka was about to sit the clothes she was going to purchase on the counter before the Asian cashier, Constance brushed passed her and pulled a thick bankroll of hundred dollar bills from out of her purse. She popped the rubber-band and shuffled through the bills as the cashier rang her up. Once Constance was given the total, she peeled off a pair of Benjamin Franklins and dropped them on the counter.

"It's called paying your own way, something you may not never know nothing about." Constance looked at her like she was a peasant and she was the Queen Bitch. Beyonce's *'Bow down'* played in her head at that moment.

I know when you were little girls/You dreamt of being in my world

Don't forget it, don't forget it/Respect that, bow down bitches

I took some time to live my life/But don't think I'm just his little wife

Don't get it twisted, get it twisted/This my shit, bow down bitches

Constance took her change from the cashier and dropped it into her purse. She slipped on her designer shades, flipped her locks, and sashayed toward the door.

Eureka didn't even have a comeback for what she had just laid down. All she could do was smirk and nod.

"You got that, bitch. You got that," she smiled.

Chapter 16
Three days later

The living room was dark save for the blue glow illumination from the 100" 3D flat-screen. Eureka sat on the sectional sofa with her fist propped up against her head, nodding off to sleep. Each time her head would drop, she'd throw it back up and look around blinking her eyes. She looked at Anton and he was lying in a fetal position with his arm tucked under his chin. His eyes were closed and his mouth was wide open, leaking drool that had pooled on his arm and dried. Hearing someone coming through the door that led out to the garage, She looked up to see Fear coming. He was wearing a navy blue hoodie, matching jeans, and Timberland boots. He moved briskly closing the door shut and locking it.

"Hey," she waved.

Fear didn't say a mothafucking thing, he kept it moving. It was like she wasn't even there. As if she was a ghost. He hastily walked toward the hallway. The glow of the flat-screen TV flickered a blue light on and off of him as the objects on it moved about. It was through these animated flickers that Eureka made out the .9mm in his hand and the specks of blood on his Timbs. She wondered what the hell was going on and curiously rose from the sofa and shook Anton awake.

"Watts up?" He sat up, rubbing his eye.

"Come get in bed upstairs," she said, picking up the remote control and killing the flat-screen.

She tossed the remote control back onto the coffee table and ushered Anton up the stairs. Once he climbed into bed, she draped a blanket over him and kissed him on the temple.

She then stepped out into the hallway, closing the door shut quietly. With the stealth of a cat burglar, Eureka approached the bathroom door. As she drew closer, she could her him wincing in pain. Cautiously, she stuck her head inside of the bathroom. Fear had just sat his .9mm on the sink and pulled his hoodie over his head. Beneath the hoodie he wore a bulletproof vest. As silent as a grave, she pushed the bathroom door open and entered. She stepped forward and he tensed up, feeling someone at his rear. With a movement so swift it registered as blurs, Fear snatched his .9mm from off of the sink and whipped around ready to leave somebody on a cold slab in the morgue. Eureka was startled when he pointed that .9mm at her. She hadn't a clue on what he was going to do next.

"I'm sorry for barging in," she apologized. "I just wanted to check to see if you were alright."

"I'm good, Reka," he winced, sitting his .9mm back on the sink. "Just a lil' banged up, is all."

He sat the .9mm down on the sink and began unstrapping the bulletproof vest.

"Here, let me help you." Eureka got down on her knees before Fear, looking up at his bulletproof vest. There were four scrunched metal bullets stuck to the bulletproof vest. One by one, she plucked each one of the bullets free and sat them on the sink. Eureka then went about the task of removing the bulletproof vest. Pulling the vest from his body, she saw four bruises where the bullets would have penetrated if not for him wearing a vest. The wounds were bluish red and looked like tenderized meat. She grimaced seeing the lumped bruises on his body.

"Where's Constance?" he asked."

"I think she's in the bedroom asleep," she told him. "Do you want me to go get her?"

"Nah." Fear shook his head, wincing. "Do me a favor, Reka. Look up into the medicine cabinet and grab that bottle of Tylenol 3 for me."

Eureka retrieved the bottle and gave him two pills to take. He then turned on the faucet, leaned over into the sink, and splashed water into his mouth to wash the pills down. While he was doing this, Eureka was rifling through the cabinet for something to treat his bruises. Coming across a tube of Scar Zone bruise cream, she took it down and removed its cap. She squeezed some of the cream out on two fingers and turned to Fear.

"Stand up so I can rub this ointment on you."

He stood with his back to the door as she got down on her knees before him, gently rubbing the cream into his bruises. His forehead wrinkled and he clenched his jaws from soreness. Tilting his head back, he moaned in pain.

Unbeknownst to them, Constance was peeking in through the crack of the door. Only she didn't see what was actually happening. What she saw was Eureka down on her knees giving Fear some Five Star Top while he stood with his head back moaning in delight. Constance's eyes misted and obscured her vision. Her bottom lip quivered and her heart felt as if it were crumbling inside of her chest like a stale cookie. She suddenly felt nauseated and her jaws swelled. She could feel her dinner threatening to erupt from her esophagus.

Hastily, she slapped a hand over her mouth and ran down the hallway. She hurried down the staircase, holding onto the railing as she went along. She leapt over the last three steps onto the floor, darted to the front door, and snatched it open. She tripped over the threshold and fell on her palms and knees. She crawled off of the porch as fast as she could, heading toward the lawn. Once she reached the lawn, she threw her head back and her cheeks puffed up. She brought her head back down and a nasty pinkish, green goop with chunks in it came spilling from out of her mouth.

Constance threw up until she was dry heaving. The thought of Fear being with someone else made her sick to her stomach. She hated to think that someone could swoop in and whisk him away. She was frightened. If Fear cut her loose, then she would be left in the world all alone.

Her father sold her, her mother was murdered and her family disowned her once they found out that she was a whore. Where could she go? Who could she turn to? Most importantly, who would love her? Hell, who would want to love her for that matter, she was a broken woman. Mentally scarred and emotionally disturbed. She had a hell of a lot of baggage, who would help her carry it? Who would be receptive to who she is? With Fear gone, she'd be forced to start all over again. Constance fell to the lawn on her side and rolled over onto her back, staring up at the twinkling stars in the black sky.

I know this bitch don't actually think that I'ma lie down and just let her take my nigga from me. If that's what she's thinking then she's got life fucked up. I ain't going out like that. Nah, I'ma make sure she closes her eyes for a nap that she'll never wake up from.

She picked herself up from the lawn and headed back inside of the house to clean herself up. She had a lot of things on her mind like. How she was going to kill Eureka was one of them.

*****

Fear leaned back on the commode with his head tilted back against the wall and his hands resting on his thighs.

"You alright?" she asked concerned, seeing that his eyes were narrowed into slits.

"Yeah, codeine gotta nigga feeling drowsy than a mothafucka." Fear admitted with a slight smirk, closing his eyes and dozing off.

Eureka grinned. She looked down and saw the specks of blood on his Timberland boots again. A line deepened on her forehead as she wondered what kind of shit he was into. Question after question racked her mind but she decided to save them all for later when he was responsive.

"Come on, let me help you into the bedroom." She grabbed his hand and the texture of his fingertips felts funny to her, like beef jerky. She turned his hand palm up and noticed that his thumb and finger tips had been burned off. More questions racked her mind as she grabbed his other hand and turned it palm up. They were singed too. She turned his hand back over to the black side and saw *L.O.E* tattooed between his thumb and index finger.

Suddenly, a cell phone rang and vibrated. She looked down and saw a dim light illuminating inside of the pocket of his jeans as it slightly shook. Curious, she cautiously stuck her hand into his pocket as she kept a close eye on him. She pulled the cell phone free and flipped it open. She pressed 'answer' and moved to bring it to her ear when his strong hand grasped her wrist. Eureka looked up startled, making eye contact with a pair of soulless eyes. Fear brought his other hand around and took the cell phone from her. He released her wrist, but kept his eyes on her as he spoke into the cell phone.

"Mission accomplished."

He disconnected the call, flipped the cell phone closed and rose to his feet. Eureka took a step back thinking that he was about to make a move. Fear slipped his cell phone into his pocket, picked up his .9mm from the sink and grabbed his bulletproof vest from the edge of the bathtub. She looked from the specks of blood on his boots, the gun in his hand, the burns on his finger tips and finally the bulletproof vest. It all tied into each other and made sense to Eureka. Fear was a hit-man.

"So now you know our secret. Constance and I are contract killaz. That's our business. You and your brother are free to leave. I only ask that you keep our secret."

He stood there as silent as a grave, waiting for her response.

"Your secret is safe with me. I swear on my father's grave."

"Thanks for taking care of me."

Eureka nodded. She watched as he ambled toward the door, but before he could disappear through it she called after him. He turned around, holding his .9mm in one hand and his bulletproof vest in the other. His face was solemn, void of emotion, but from the look in his eyes you could tell that he was drowsy.

"If it's alright with you, I'd like to continue living here 'til I figure out my next move."

Fear nodded and continued on out of the door. Eureka sat down on the commode and scooped up the scrunched bullets into her palm. She bounced the bullets around in her palm thinking, *Boy, you think you know someone. Who would have thought?*

*****

Fear entered his bedroom to find Constance lying asleep on her side under the sheets. He used the blue glow illuminating from the flat-screen to find his way around the bedroom. He stored his bulletproof vest in the back of the closet and kicked off his Timberland boots.

He then kneeled down to the floor of the closet and flipped back a flap of carpet. After taking a cautious glance over his shoulder and seeing that she was still asleep, he punched in the combination to his digital safe. Fear threw the door of the safe open and dropped his .9mm inside, on top of stacks of money.

He then stashed his clothes inside of a black garbage bag, along with his Timbs. He threw on a tank top and a pair of sweatpants, grabbed the bag and took it downstairs. After he got the fire going in the fireplace, he tossed the black garbage bag into it. He then took a step back and sparked up an L, watching the flames lick away at his clothes and boots. Once they had perished, he went back upstairs into his bedroom. He killed the flat-screen and slipped into bed. He glanced at the digital clock on the dresser. It was 12:05 AM. He then closed his eyes for a night's rest. The last image that passed through his mind was Eureka's face.

Chapter 17
Three hours later

The night had settled and all that could be heard was the late night traffic. The occasional car would zoom pass the house, but the noise wasn't enough to wake anyone. Constance's eyes peeled open and she looked around. She turned over in bed and found Fear with his back to her. She looked over his shoulder and saw his eyes closed and his mouth slightly open. He was asleep. Needing to be sure that the Sandman had taken him, Constance shook him gently and called his name. When he didn't respond she eased herself from under the covers and out of the bed.

She slipped her feet into her Timberland boots and slowly pulled open the dresser drawer. When the drawer made a creak midway, she stopped and looked over her shoulder. Seeing that Fear hadn't made a move, she continued with the drawer until it was all of the way out. Constance dipped her hand into drawer and when it came back up it was clutching her .45 automatic. She held the .45 in one hand and reached back into the drawer with the other. She brought the silencer she'd taken from the drawer to the barrel of her weapon and began screwing it on. Constance kept an eye on him as she screwed the silencer onto her .45. When the silencer was screwed on tight, she rose to her feet and snuck out of the bedroom keeping an eye on Fear on her way out.

She crept down the hallway toward the Eureka and Anton's bedroom. Holding her silenced .45 up to her shoulder, she slowly turned the doorknob.

Click! Clack! Click! Clack!

The door was locked. *Fuck,* Constance mouthed with a wrinkled forehead and scrunched up nose. She lowered her .45 automatic to her side and hustled down the staircase, heading inside of the kitchen. Entering the kitchen, she approached the door that lead out into the garage and opened it. She flipped on the light-switch and gave a quick scan of the area. When she located the opened containers of rat poison in the corners of the garage, she smiled wickedly.

*****

Later that morning

Malvo sat at the kitchen table across from Crunch. He nervously smoked a cigarette and watched the cell phone ring for the thousandth time as it danced across the table. He shook his head regretfully wishing that he'd never entrusted Ronny with the task of bringing back his drugs.

It had been nearly three weeks since he had seen or heard from him. He'd called his cell phone a million times and it went directly to voicemail. Once Malvo realized that Ronny wasn't going to answer, he called his girlfriend, his side chick, and his mother every hour on the hour. All of them claimed to not have seen or heard from Ronny for as long as he had. With that in mind, the gears of Malvo's mental began to turn. He hated to believe that Ronny had given him a great big fuck you and ran off with his dope. He'd been loyal to him since the day he'd put a package in his hand, so he didn't want to think that he'd crossed him. But all of the signs were leading him to believe just that.

The cell phone stopped ringing and thirty missed calls appeared on the display screen. As soon as Malvo reached for the cell phone it rang with a text message. His forehead creased as he wondered who'd left him the text. Flipping the cell phone open, he took a gander at the text message. It was sent by an unavailable number but he knew who it was.

U R A DEAD MAN.

"Shit!" Malvo shook his head. He then threw the cell phone at the wall, breaking it. Sitting up in his chair, he mashed his square out in the ashtray and cleared his throat. He looked Crunch in his eyes, "I want you to comb the streets for Ronny. If you find him with my dope..." Crunch sat there staring at Malvo and waiting for the next word to leave his lips. A moment later he finished his order. "...kill 'em."

Crunch nodded and rose from out of the chair. He tucked his banger on his waistline and headed to the door. He pulled the door open and was about to cross the threshold when Malvo called him back. Crunch threw his head back like 'What's up?'

"Be mindful of his face," he told him. "I want to give his family an open casket funeral, at least."

Crunch nodded and stepped through the door with a heavy heart. It pained him to have to kill his best friend but he'd sworn an oath to Malvo when he'd put him on and he'd be damned if he betrayed it.

*****

Eureka lay in bed asleep with a twitching nose as the aroma of steak, scrambled eggs and toast invaded her nostrils and caused her stomach to grumble with hunger. Her eyes fluttered open and she sat up in bed, wiping the scum from out of the corners of her eyes. She looked to the window and saw the sun shining through the slight openings of the blinds, illuminating the bedroom. The day was warm and beautiful. She could hear the birds chirping, a lawnmower running and kids playing. She grabbed her piece from under her pillow and sat up in bed, shaking Anton awake. He turned over in bed, looking at her and rubbing his eyes.

"Rise and shine, my boy," she said groggily.

Anton sat up in bed, "Something smells good."

"Yeah, somebody's over the stove," she told him. "Let's go see what's on the menu."

"Bet."

"Good morning," they said after each other as they entered the kitchen.

Constance gave them a nod and took a bite of her eggs.

"Good morning." Fear held a mug of steaming black coffee while reading the morning newspaper. "Your plates are inside of the microwave. Pull up a chair," he nodded to the two empty chairs at the table.

Eureka took her and Anton's plates out of the microwave and sat down at the kitchen table. She removed the foil from off of her plate and admired the breakfast before her. She couldn't wait to dig in. Constance wiped her mouth with a napkin and balled it up. Dropping the balled up napkin beside her plate, she picked up her glass of orange juice. She took a sip and a devilish smile formed on her lips as she watched Eureka gather eggs on her fork.

Uh huh, bitch, Bon Appétit, Constance thought.

Eureka didn't know it, but this could very well be her last supper.

*****

That night...

Boom!

The basement door swung open from a strong kick, bouncing off of the wall. Two men in blood stained ponchos and splotched black leather gloves dragged a battered Ronny down the staircase. Ronny's head was swollen to the size of a pumpkin, his right-eye was swollen, and his nose was broken. His face and body were wet with blood and perspiration. He had hung chained from the ceiling inside of a chop shop and used as a punching bag by his kidnappers. Every half hour his kidnappers would take beer and cigarette breaks then get back to beating him to a pulp. Ronny winced with every wheezing

181

breath that he took, feeling his broken ribs. He had been to hell and back again, and wanted nothing more than a bullet through his head to put him out of his misery.

Once they reached the bottom of the staircase, one of the kidnappers left the other holding up Ronny while he secured a light. There was some shuffling around in the darkness as things were being moved around and sometime later a lamp light came on. The light's illumination wasn't much but it gave them just enough to see what they were about to do.

The kidnappers drug Ronny over to a rickety wooden chair that looked like it would collapse under a considerable amount of pressure. Together, they hoisted him upon the rickety chair. One of the kidnappers stepped upon a tattered milk crate and pulled the noose down from the ceiling, looping it around Ronny's neck. He jumped down and went to stand beside his cohort. Hearing the squeaks of the wooden steps as some descended them, the kidnappers turned around to see a tall Caucasian man, wearing slicked back blonde hair and an expensive white suit.

The Caucasian man walked between the two kidnappers and up to Ronny. He looked up at him with a pair of unforgiving eyes. He extended a hand decorated with diamond and gold rings toward Ronny's lips, snatching off the duct-tape and causing him to grimace.

"I'll be the first to admit, you have big balls, my friend." Expensive suit said with a thick Russian accent, "Big gigantic balls. The size of boulders." He showed the size with his hands. "It's just too bad you weren't born Russian, Ronny?"

"Fuck—fuck Russia," Ronny spat heatedly. "Russia can suck my big black, Mandingo dick!" He spat on the Russian, speckling his face and his expensive suit with blood.

The Russian chuckled as he pulled out his handkerchief and patted his face dry. "Fucking nigger!" He tucked the handkerchief back into the pocket of his suit. He whipped out a pair of black leather gloves, put them on, and flexed his fingers in them. Keeping his begrudging eyes on Ronny and holding out his hand to one of the kidnappers, he said, "Pistol."

The kidnapper pulled a Desert Eagle from his waistline, cocked the slide, and smacked it down in the Russian's palm.

"Where's your boss?" The Russian asked like he did earlier.

"I guess you're hard of hearing, so I'll say it again, *fuck you!*"

Blam!

The front wooden rod was blown in half and the front legs of the rickety chair tilted inward. The Russian looked up at Ronny for his answer now.

"Fuck you!"

Blam!

The back wooden rod was blown off this time, and the rear wood legs tilted inwards. The chair was weaker now.

Ronny's eyes zipped back and forth about his surroundings, following the hooded entity with the scythe floating around the basement. The Grim Reaper was lingering near and he was petrified, but he didn't want anything less than a gangster's death.

"Fuck you, mothafucka!" Ronny shouted viciously, making red spittle fly.

Blam! Blam!

The third shot tore the right front leg from beneath the rickety chair while a forth tore off the rear left leg. The chair now had two legs holding it up. A dark spot expanded in the crotch of Ronny's jeans and a yellow stream ran down his leg, wetting the chair's seat. Ronny's bare feet scrambled upon the wet surface as they tried to right themselves. He began to lose his equilibrium and that caused the noose to tighten around his neck, stifling his throat. His eyes bulged as the rope bit into his throat and he felt the equivalent of a carpet burn around his neck. Ronny's eyes turned glassy and veins snaked up his temple. He sucked in what little air he could in sips as he struggled to stay alive. Although, Ronny discovered a foundation at the balls of his feet. The chair still shook madly having only two legs to support it. All that shit he was popping had come to a halt.

The Russian smiled wickedly having seen Ronny struggling to balance himself on the loose seat of the chair. "You feel that, that chill? It feels like a cold December breeze, don't it? That's the icy hands of death trying to pull you into the afterlife." He analyzed as Ronny's legs shook uncontrollably and the yellow pool between his feet grew. "Today you die, unless you want to tell me where Malvo is?"

Ronny's head shook as if it were vibrating and tears spilled from the corners of his eyes. The noose had become tighter around his neck and he could feel himself about to lose his balance on the seat.

Ronny shook his head no to the best of his ability.

The Russian sucked his teeth. "Stupid, stupid, man," he said, as he massaged the bridge of his nose.

He pointed the Desert Eagle at one of the surviving legs. Once he shot it out, the chair would collapse and lynch Ronny from the ceiling. "One last time, my friend," the Russian said callously. He was so angry with Ronny's stubbornness; his eyes looked like two small embers. He clenched his jaws and revealed his chipped front tooth.

Seeing the look in the Russian's eyes, Ronny knew that it was do or die. The next words that left his lips would determine whether he was given life or death. Ronny could literally see the demons of hell dancing before his eyes as well as the small fires on the ground that licked the air. The scenery darkened and he could smell burning flesh. His surroundings were becoming more and more like the backdrop of the place that all rotten souls were sent.

Ronny's lips peeled apart to give his answer but before he could utter a word, a gun was fired and the chair collapsed beneath his feet.

To Be Continued...

The Devil Wears Timbs II

Baptized In Unholy Waters

AVAILABLE NOW BY TRANAY ADAMS

The Devil Wears Timbs 1-5

Bury Me A G 1-3

Tyson's Treasure 1-2

Treasure's Pain

A South Central Love Affair

Me And My Hittas 1- 6

The Last Real Nigga Alive 1-3

Fangeance

Fearless

COMING SOON BY TRANAY ADAMS

The Devil Wears Timbs 6: Just Like Daddy

A Hood Nigga's Blues

Bloody Knuckles

Billy Bad Ass

Tranay Adams

The Devil Wears Timbs

CPSIA information can be obtained
at www.ICGtesting.com
Printed in the USA
LVHW082348200721
693167LV00009BA/508